tHe chuRch iNvisiBle

Also by Nick Page
Blue
The Map: Making the Bible Meaningful, Accessible, Practical
street life (coauthored with Rob Lacey)

A JouRney iNto the FutuRe
of the UK ChuRch

tHe chuRch iNvisiBle

NicK PaGe

ZONDERVAN™

GRAND RAPIDS, MICHIGAN 49530 USA

ZONDERVAN™

The Church Invisible
Copyright © 2004 by Nick Page

Requests for information should be addressed to:

Zondervan, *Grand Rapids, Michigan 49530*

Nick Page asserts the moral right to be identified as the author of this work.

Library of Congress Cataloging-in-Publication Data

Page, Nick, 1961–
    The church invisible : a journey into the future of the UK church / Nick
Page.—1st ed.
       p. cm.
    Includes bibliographical references and index.
    ISBN 0-310-25029-3
    1. Church buildings—Fiction. 2. Church membership—Fiction.
    3. Twenty-first century—Fiction. 4. England—Fiction. I. Title.
    PR6116.A36 C48 2004
    823'.926dc22

                                         2003024158

Some of this material originally appeared in *Christianity and Renewal* magazine. I am grateful to them for the permission to reprint it here.

The website addresses recommended throughout this book are offered as a resource to you. These websites are not intended in any way to be or imply an endorsement on the part of Zondervan, nor do we vouch for their content for the life of this book.

Interior design by Beth Shagene

Printed in the United States of America

04 05 06 07 08 09 10 /❖ DC/ 10 9 8 7 6 5 4 3 2 1

→ • ←

This book is dedicated to Lydia.
Whoever she is.

coNteNts

tHe chuRch iNvisiBle

a Nasty sHocK

The church in the UK was bleeding to death.

I think I finally realised this at around 8.05 pm on a sultry, sticky evening in July. I was sitting in a meeting in Oxford; a meeting called by a national organisation and entitled 'The Future for the Church: It's Not as Bad as It Seems'. Unfortunately, it probably *was* as bad as it seemed.

Indeed, it might even be worse, for, as I listened to the statistics and looked at the people around me, I began to doubt that the church actually had a future. The church in the UK was an elderly, frail, terminally ill patient, haemorrhaging people at a frightening rate. Children were leaving by their thousands. Families were staying away. The elderly were dying and not being replaced.

And while the patient was fading fast, the doctors were bickering about the diagnosis. Instead of the solutions I had come to discover and discuss, I was presented with a mixture of lame excuses and blind optimism. One vicar stood up and disagreed with the way the figures were collected: 'I have lots of people coming into my church for funerals,' she said. 'What about them?' Another rose – albeit somewhat slowly – and informed us all that he had no intention of changing his time-honoured ways, despite the fact that half his congregation had left.

'Our church remains untouched by progress,' he said proudly. Some people even applauded him.

There was a moment of excitement when a young, energetic pastor rose to tell us how his church was growing rapidly; everyone was impressed until it became evident that his church was filling up with all those who had left the previous speaker's congregation. Another minister stood up and complained that the problem was that most of his congregation were dead. Whether he meant spiritually or physically I wasn't sure; perhaps it didn't matter.

And so it went on. Speaker after speaker turning away from the facts, taking refuge in ever more desperate hopes and assertions. There were some good things, it is true. There were welcome stories of people becoming Christians, of lives being changed. But overall it was like watching a large number of ostriches sticking their heads into an even larger bucket of sand.

In the end I left feeling more depressed than ever. I wanted to share their hope, their optimism, I wanted to bury my head in the same, welcoming bucket. But I couldn't. The reality was that the church was bleeding to death. What signs of life there were, were little more than the nervous twitches of a mortally wounded beast.

'Cheer up, mate,' said the bus driver as I climbed on board. 'It might never happen.'

'It already has,' I replied.

As the bus sped through the countryside at a speed which would have made Michael Schumacher tremble, I thought of my daughters back at home, asleep in their beds. Would they grow up in a country where no-one believes what I believed? Would there even be a church for them in twenty years' time? And what would our country be like when no-one goes to church anymore?

The evening was hot, oppressive. The village lay silent all around me. I stepped down from the bus, crossed the village square, and stood staring at the church, the building which had been a part of the village for many centuries, at the thick wooden door which had stood open every Sunday for six hundred years, and which, I was afraid would someday close forever. Admittedly, at my church we were doing better than most. The church was growing, the vicar committed to evangelism, the place was alive. But it was only a drop in the ocean. And it wasn't going to be enough.

Overhead there was a rumble of thunder. There was no wind and the air was sluggish and greasy with heat. I turned away from the church.

'I wish I could know for sure,' I said to myself. 'I wish I knew what was going to happen.'

Then, it happened. Time seemed to stand still; the world seemed to stop, as if someone had pressed the 'pause' button. There was a brief moment – a nanosecond – of total, utter silence, during which I could see the village square lit up, caught in the flash of a giant camera. Then the silence was replaced by a noise, a huge, thundering roar, and I was caught up in a cataract of fire and flame. The air around me crackled, and exploded; my body was sliced through by a huge, dry, roaring blast of heat. In that moment I knew, with an almost mystical clarity, exactly what it felt like to be a steak-and-kidney pie at the moment when the microwave is switched on.

Then everything went black.

→•←

In the darkness there was a voice: 'Stay still, I'm scanning.'

I opened my eyes and shut them again. It felt like the cast of *Riverdance* were tap dancing on my eyeballs. Everything hurt. My head, my arms, my legs ... even my hair. There was a horrible taste in my mouth, a metallic, acid taste, as if I had been drinking water from a rusty tin cup.

I tried to lift my head, and my brain started to do the conga out of my ears.

'Lie still,' said the voice. 'You've obviously had a nasty shock.'

I opened my eyes. My eyeballs gave one scream of agony and then went on strike. Whimpering with the pain, I shut my eyes and tried again. After a few attempts at opening my eyelids I managed to get the pain down from the 'complete agony' to the 'intensely painful' level. The light still hurt, but at least the world had stopped shuddering.

'What happened?' There was a man kneeling over me. He had a shock of unruly black hair and was wearing a pair of mirrored sunglasses, over which two bushy eyebrows quivered, looking like two caterpillars performing a strange mating ritual. For a moment it almost appeared as if the light in his glasses was making tiny letters and images. Small specks of information seemed to dance across the lenses, like light sparkling on a green river.

'Well, I think I must have been struck by lightning,' I said. 'There was this thunder and then everything went dark ...'

He looked at me curiously.

'We haven't had any thunder here, Citizen,' he said. 'It's been a dry, sunny day. We haven't had rain for weeks.'

'Well, I don't know where you've been,' I muttered. 'It poured only yesterday. And tonight the clouds were gathering ...'

He shook his head. The green light in his sunglasses flickered and coalesced into strange, mesmerising patterns.

'Wait a minute,' I said. The sunglasses had alerted me to something that I should have noticed straightaway. 'Tonight . . . ,' I muttered. 'It's not tonight.' I tried to sit up. I'd had a sense all along that something was wrong, and now I could identify what it was: it was sunny. It was daytime. All around me, lit by bright sunshine, were the familiar buildings – the pub, the village hall, the church. The night had disappeared completely, to be replaced by sunshine, gentle birdsong, and dappled shadows on the pavement of the square. 'It's daylight,' I stammered. 'That's wrong! Should be night-time.'

The man kneeling over me looked anxious. At least I assumed he looked anxious. It was difficult to see behind the sunglasses. But his eyebrows looked concerned. 'Stay still,' he said. 'You've obviously had a nasty shock.'

'No. I was hit by lightning . . . it was night-time. Dark.' I rubbed my head. Then the solution occurred to me. 'I must have lain here all night,' I said. 'I was obviously hit by lightning and then lay here. And nobody noticed me because they were all too busy trying to escape the rain.'

'I keep telling you, citizen,' said the man, his eyebrows moving from 'concerned' to 'mildly alarmed'. 'We haven't had any rain for days.' The man stood up. 'Anyway, I don't think there's any harm been done,' he said. 'Nothing's registering on the scans.'

'What scans?'

'The diog-web of course,' he said. 'My Putershades say everything's okay.'

There was a pause. 'I'm sorry,' I said, 'But you appear to be speaking fluent gibberish. Your what?'

He looked at me as though I was mad. 'Putershades, of course.' He pointed at the sunglasses and this time I was sure. Small letters and numbers were flickering on the lenses, green lights, dancing against the darkness. 'Surely you have a pair.'

'No ... no I don't. They're great.' Despite the pain, my inbuilt, masculine love of gadgets kicked in. 'Where can you buy them?'

He, and his eyebrows, laughed. 'You don't *buy* them, citizen,' he said. 'You get given them. When you apply for your Citizen Card.'

'This is all wrong ...,' I muttered. 'Putershades. Citizen cards. This is some kind of joke.' I looked around the square. Then I noticed it. The most wrong thing in a list of very wrong things. 'Wait a minute ...,' I said, pointing past the man. 'What's happened to the church?'

He looked around.

'What do you mean?'

'Well it ... it's got more doors. Four.'

He looked at me as though I were stupid. 'Of course. How else are the residents supposed to get in?'

'But it looks like it's been turned into houses.'

There was a pause. I squinted at the building through the fog of pain that was clouding my head. There were four steel doors set into the side of the church, there were window boxes under the windows and large golden coloured dishes on the top which seemed to be some kind of TV or satellite receivers. There were four doorbells. Then I saw the sign on the side of the building:

St Jude's Sheltered Housing. Nos. 1–4.
No hawkers. No canvassers.
No virtual door-to-door salesmen.

'Typical!' I shouted angrily. 'The vicar never consults anyone. I thought it was bad enough when he launched his sermon series on "Brassware of the Old Testament", but now he's sold the church.'

My companion looked at me and smiled. 'Citizen,' he said quietly. 'It was turned into houses twenty years ago. Most of the churches are houses now.'

'Look, I've had enough of this,' I said. 'Thanks for your help, but since you're obviously mad, I'd better go and sort this out for myself.'

I rose unsteadily to my feet and made my way towards the church. The ground wobbled under my feet, as though I was trying to walk on a trampoline. With relief, I made it to the first door, about halfway along the wall of the church. It was a sleek, steel panel, set neatly into the old stone. I looked for the bell, but there was none.

'Hello?' I shouted, knocking on the metal plate. 'Is there anyone at home? Hello?'

Suddenly, with an almost imperceptible hiss, the door slid open.

'Do come in,' said a stern, slightly elderly voice. 'I've been expecting you.'

I stepped across the threshold and into a brightly lit room. There was a sofa and chairs set against the far wall, and the opposite wall was a strange, silvery colour that seemed to move and dance before me.

'Hello, Nick. You're looking well.'

I looked around. There, emerging from a side passage was a woman. She had light grey hair, pulled back into rather a severe ponytail. Her face was tanned and her blue eyes stared at me in a disconcertingly direct way. There was something of the old-fashioned schoolmistress about her. She wore what appeared to be a pair of dungarees made of a silver, padded material. She was carrying a tray of tea.

'I imagine you could do with this,' she said. 'You must be thirsty.' I nodded. 'Now,' she said, 'I seem to remember it was two sugars, wasn't it?'

This was all getting too much for me. 'Er ... look,' I said. 'I'm not trying to be rude or anything, but how do you know my name? Who are you? And what are you doing living in the church?'

She set the tea tray down.

'To answer in reverse order. I'm living in the church because it's been turned into housing. After all, no-one was using it for anything else. My name is Lydia. And I know you because I used to sit in this church as a young woman and listen to you preach.'

There was a pause.

'Exactly what have you got in those tea bags?' I asked.

She laughed.

'Nick,' she said. 'Twenty years ago I had a vision. I dreamed that one day I would be living here and you would come to visit me. I didn't know then what that vision meant, but I've had it on the same day every year since. As regular as clockwork. Even after you died, the vision persisted. Twenty times that picture has come to me. It came again last night. And today, at last, there you are.' She handed me my tea. 'Punctuality was never your strong point.'

I closed my eyes. There was a word there that was troubling me; a phrase she had used. A little tiny fact. Then it hit me.

'WHAT DO YOU MEAN "AFTER I DIED"?' I yelled.

'There's no need to get upset. No-one lives forever. You were seventy, after all.'

I shook my head. 'No I'm not. I mean I wasn't. I mean ... I'm not dead.'

'Yes you are. Come with me.'

She waved a hand and the huge, shimmering window overlooking the churchyard slid back silently into a recess in the wall. From outside drifted in some old, familiar sensations: newly mown grass, the scent of lilac, the sound of birdsong. We walked out into the graveyard and down the gravel path. To my right was a large yew tree and into my mind swum a memory of planting the same tree, the same tree only so much smaller, to mark the millennium. The graveyard looked more or less as I remembered it, unless . . . unless, were there more graves, or was I imagining it?

We turned off the path and padded over mossy grass to a pale sand-coloured headstone standing under a tall chestnut. On it, in large, deep letters, was written:

NICK PAGE
1961–2031

'Nick,' said Lydia softly. 'You're in the future. You died nine years ago.'

Dear Miles,

It was good to talk to you the other day. You were quite right, of course; things have been difficult for me recently. I should have known better than to try to pull the wool over your eyes; you are one of the few people I have ever met who, when he asks 'how are you?' really means it.

People are very kind, but I know what they're thinking. They're thinking, 'It's been nearly a year now. The old man should stop moping and try to move on.' Perhaps they're right. But move on to where? And with what purpose?

Well, perhaps that was why you thought of me when you were looking over this manuscript. And I have to admit that, at first glance, I am intrigued.

As I understand it, the situation is as follows:

1) The manuscript you sent me is – or rather it purports to be – an account of one man's visit to the future. Its hero claims that he has been projected into the future, where he was shown around what was left of the church in the UK.

2) The author – your friend Nick Page – remains adamant that the whole thing is true.

3) He is now refusing to talk about it any further. Given, as you say 'he rarely shuts up for more than a minute', this has caused you some alarm.

So what you want from me is an analysis of his arguments and a response as to the veracity of the tale. You wish, in short, to know whether it's a load of what my young nephew calls 'porkies'.

It's certainly a novel suggestion. Various well-meaning individuals have suggested hobbies or evening-classes to help me 'snap out of it'. I have been urged to take up watercolour painting, or cookery, or even jujitsu. But so far, no one has suggested I amuse myself by examining the writings of a middle-aged author who has apparently been projected into the future. I'm not sure they do an evening class in that.

Quite why you thought I would be the right person to comment on this is beyond me. I am neither a statistician nor a sociologist. And the only thing I know about predictions of the future is that they are almost invariably wrong. As you know, my special area of interest has always been early Church History.

However, as I say, I am intrigued. So I have decided to take you up on your offer. Perhaps, after all, the only way to understand this vision of the future is to analyse it in the light of the past.

So, yes. I will read the manuscript and give you my response. Indeed, I already have started doing it. I've started by playing detective. I'm reminded of all those television programmes that Caroline used to watch; all classical music and bodies everywhere.

First, I have identified the conference which Page claims to have attended. This was an evening meeting and was part of a series entitled 'Whither Church?' (Actually, the promotional leaflet I have is actually entitled 'Wither Church?' which seems something of a Freudian slip. Or a Freudian typo, at least.)

As to whether he actually attended that evening's session, that has been harder to verify. It was a free evening, so no tickets were issued. However, I did speak to one of the ladies who helped with the organisation and she did recall a 'balding man with a goatee beard who kept muttering to himself and left looking angry' – which is probably as close to a definite sighting as we're going to get. (As I recall, from the one time I met him, he has a vandyke beard and not a goatee, but I don't suppose you're worried about that level of detail.) Anyway, we know he went to the event, and from what you have found out we know that he collapsed in the village square later that night. Several people in Page's home village can attest to that fact.

So, thus far he appears to be telling the truth.

Beyond these facts, of course, we cannot really go. So from now on I'll focus on the content of the manuscript; his message, as it were. And, given that he starts with pronouncements about the church, I thought I would take a look at the statistics myself.

So, let me try to simplify things. Here, as I see it, are the key facts, the really important ones you need to know.

1. The Church Is Getting Smaller

· Between 1980 and 2000 nearly 1.9 million people left the British church. 1800 people leave each week. That's one every six minutes.
· In the last ten years, the rate of decline has increased.

2. The Church Is Getting Older

· In 1980, the average Anglican was aged 36. Now the average age is 47. For every 100 children in the Church of England in 1930, there are now 9.
· In 1989, 19% of churchgoers were 65 or over. By 1998 that figure had risen to 25%.

Given these facts, you would think that there would be much more of an outcry in the church. You would think that there would be a much more strategic response. But that is not the case. I am an old man with a level of arthritis in my bones; but I believe I could react faster than most of the denominations.

The Church of England

Current situation: Declining rapidly – a 30% decline in the last twenty years, dropping from 1.3 million people in 1980 to 960,000 in the year 2000. Child attendance is declining at double the rate of the adult attendance. The denomination is riven with splits; not just on the homosexual clergy, but also on women priests, the use of money, whether or not the church should be established, the shape of liturgy, the ordination and training of clergy and arguments about the power and authority of bishops.

The response: Well, they tried a new way of counting their membership, but all these new figures show really is that the decline is ever so slightly less steep than once we thought. There are a number of organisations within the denomination working hard to promote new thinking and alternatives, and they are, belatedly recognising the need for action. The new Archbishop has talked of the Anglicans facing a 'messy' few years and of having to alter its structures to cope.

The Methodist Church

Current situation: The Methodist Church has seen a drop in membership of some 38% in the past twenty years, and a decline of 7% in membership in the past three years alone. Worldwide it is healthy, but some prominent Methodists have warned that the UK branch has five years to reform or die. It's been around 300 years, but whether it will last another 30 is not so certain.

The Response: They have appointed a national general secretary to raise their profile and they are also exploring the possibilities of a merger with the Anglicans. This won't be straightforward: Methodists have women bishops (or district chairmen, to be precise), and a previous attempt at unity in the seventies collapsed after Anglo-Catholic opposition. Nevertheless, the move does seem to have gathered some momentum. However, given the dire state of the Anglican Church, this might not be what you call 'a long-term solution'.

The Catholics

Current Situation: No denomination is declining faster than the Catholic Church. The numbers attending the Catholic Church in Britain have declined by some 40% over the past twenty years and some 50,000 people stop attending mass each year. The authority of the church has been further eroded by a number of scandals – from child abuse by priests, to bishops arrested for hit-and-run driving. These have led to lawsuits which could cripple their work.

The Response: Shout louder. Generally, the authorities have hardened their position and attempted to reinforce orthodoxy. Some organisations and individuals are campaigning for reform and for more lay involvement, but without much evidence of success.

The Baptists

Current Situation: The only 'traditional' denomination that is growing – by around 2% in the last five years. However, when we look at the figures a bit further back, we see that the denomination has merely recovered the 2% it dropped earlier in the eighties.

The Response: The independence of individual Baptist churches gives them greater flexibility in responding to local needs and in setting new initiatives, but as a denomination they have generally been more focused and proactive. At the start of the 1990s they framed policies for future growth and engaged in some organisational reform. (They also committed themselves to an over-ambitious church planting programme, but you can't fault them for trying.)

The New Churches

Current Situation: Satisfaction bordering on smugness. The new churches – by which I mean the churches which grew out of the house church movement of the seventies and eighties – have been growing rapidly. In the past five years, they have added some 35,000 people to their numbers, a growth rate of 16%.

However, a word of caution might be advisable. Most of these churches were not in existence 20 years ago, so they are bound to exhibit growth. Anyone can speed up from a standing start; it's increasing the pace during the race that is difficult.

The Response: More of the same. The biggest question to be answered, though, is how much of the growth is what is called 'transfer growth', where Christians from other churches have simply swapped allegiance. In America some experts have claimed that up to 90% of new church members are recycled Christians from other fellowships. This may point to the inadequacies of the other churches, but it should serve as a warning not to get too excited about the increases. The fact remains that the growth in the new churches has not changed the overall picture of decline.

Other Churches

Of the other denominations, the Independent churches have dropped by 37%, the United Reformed Church by 36%; the Pentecostal church has remained almost exactly the same. The Orthodox churches have achieved a lot of growth, although this is probably due to a rise in immigration from Eastern bloc countries.

———————

By now, dear Miles, I expect you have eyestrain and brain-ache! However, I offer all these facts merely to demonstrate that, whatever the fantasies he may harbour about time travel, Page's analogy of the terminally ill patient is not so far from the truth.

Against that, of course, is one very important, very significant fact: *the church is not dead yet.*

An organisation which still claims millions of members can hardly be said to be in a 'terminal' condition. Nevertheless, the church, one feels, ought to be in more of a state of alarm than it is. It reminds me of a client of Caroline's, whom I once met at a party. An elderly, once-glamorous actress, she wore long, obviously artificial blonde hair and makeup which looked as though it had been applied by a semiqualified plasterer. She backed me into a corner and told me how she had once 'acted with Brando'. Caroline, who came to my rescue, informed me that she was, in fact, a very good actress, but one who had never come to terms with the fact that times had changed.

'If only she'd take on different parts, she could be a star again,' said Caroline. 'But she still believes that she can play the romantic heroine. She won't reinvent herself.'

That, broadly, is how I feel about the church. It backs you into a corner at parties and tells you how it was once famous. It could, like the actress, be famous again.

But reinvention is a difficult thing. As the actress could no doubt have told any bishop.

Ever yours,
Stephen

deAd agaiN

Someone was walking over my grave, and that someone was me.

I stood there, staring down at the simple, sandstone slab, bearing my name in deeply engraved gold letters. A body – my body – claimed to be lying six foot under the turf. If it was all some huge practical joke, it was remarkably well-funded. I knelt down and pulled away some ivy which had covered the base of the stone. Beneath my name and dates there was some further writing:

Here lies all we could find.
May he rest in pieces.

I leapt back, as if I had been stung.

'What does it mean, "all we could find"?' I asked, nervously.

Lydia shook her head. 'It's probably best not to know.'

'But that's me under there! What happened?'

'Trust me.' Lydia waved her hand, as if she were trying to wipe away my anxieties. 'You'd only get upset about it. And anyway, I'm sure it was virtually painless.'

'"Virtually" painless? "Virtually"? What's that supposed to mean?'

'I'm sorry. I really don't think it would be wise for me to tell you.'

I looked down at the stone. The world was spinning. Creation had gone mad. I was angry, bewildered, upset.

'And anyway,' I complained, 'I never wanted that on my gravestone. I wanted "See? I Told You I Was Ill". Or "I Demand a Second Opinion". Or . . . anything rather than that. I wanted to make people smile. I wanted my monument to have a play area for children. I wanted a bit of life . . .'

'Nick,' she said gently, 'None of that matters at the moment. Just accept it. You are in the future. You're dead. And there's absolutely nothing you can do about it.'

She took me gently by the arm.

'You've had a nasty shock,' she said. 'Now let's go and have another cup of tea, shall we?'

As we walked back into Lydia's room at the east end of the church, she asked me about what I had been doing before my apparent leap forward in time.

'You are here for a purpose,' she mused, pouring me another cup of tea. 'Do you know what that is?'

I shook my head. 'I was at a church meeting . . . a meeting about the future of the church . . . I remember thinking about the future, about my daughters. And wanting, more than I've ever wanted anything before, to know what was going to happen.'

She smiled, grimly.

'There you go then,' she said. 'That's what you are here for. You've come to find the future of the church.'

'And I've seen it,' I said. 'Sheltered accommodation. The future of the church is property development. Not so much church planting as house building.'

'Yes,' she said. 'There's been a lot of that.' She looked at me, as though weighing up my strength.

'Go on, then,' I said. 'Tell me what happened.'

So she did.

→•←

There are no village churches left now,' she said. 'There was one left up in Yorkshire, but it went a few months ago. It's a kitchen salesroom now, or a sushi bar. I forget which. All the rest have been knocked down, or turned into bars, clubs, sports halls, museums.' She gestured around her. 'Or houses.'

'But what happens when people want to get married?' I asked. 'And what about christenings or funerals?'

She smiled. 'No-one gets married any more,' she said. 'No-one makes promises these days.' She sighed. 'I often think that that was one of the main things the church had to teach people: what it meant to keep promises.'

'What about burials?'

'The government banned them several years ago, because of the shortage of land. Now everyone is biodynamically recycled.'

'Er ... I'm sorry?'

She shook her head. 'You don't want to know the details.'

'It sounds a bit like cremation ...,' I guessed.

'No,' she replied. 'I should say it's more like composting.'

'Oh.' I thought for a moment. She was right. I really *didn't* want to know the details. I tried to concentrate on the other end of the spectrum. 'What about christenings?'

'Don't be daft! How can people be welcomed into a church that no longer exists? No, all the rituals have been lost.' She shook her head. 'You know when I was young I never understood that people need ritual. I always used to despise it rather. Now, there is no ritual any more, I can see how sorely it is missed. Of course, some people still have their children christened. Mr Henderson down the other end has got the font in his living room, so people still pay him money to have their child dunked. They're trying to "rediscover" traditional England. For them it's like taking up Morris Dancing or smoking a clay pipe.'

'For many people in our day it was more or less the same,' I said.

'Perhaps. But at least there was always the hope that something would come out of that contact.'

'So what happened?' I asked. 'Where did it all go wrong? How could the church just disappear this way?'

She sighed.

'There are so many reasons,' she said. 'As you will no doubt find. But if you ask me, I think the primary reason was that we forgot how to be different.'

'What do you mean?'

'The church is here – *was* here, I should say – to show people what God is like. Didn't you used to say that yourself?'

I nodded. 'I nicked it from someone more intelligent.'

'Well anyway. Just as Israel was "invented" by God to show other nations what he was like, so the church was intended to demonstrate God to those around it. We were supposed to "be" God for these people; walking images of Jesus. I mean, those around us, they were never going to read the Bible, they were never going to read a tract or a booklet. The only way they were ever going to understand anything about God was through our example.' She looked down. 'The problem was that somewhere along the way we stopped being walking images of God and became like walking images of the world.'

'But isn't Christianity concerned with the world?'

'Of course. But look at Jesus' life. People wanted to be with him; to be like him.' She paused. 'If you ask me the fundamental problem of the church in the last decades was quite simple: no-one wanted to be like us any more. And we were too busy trying to be like them to notice.'

She went to the back of the room and rummaged around in an old box on the floor. When she returned she had a pile of old books – all from my time, many of which I had read. They were all attempting to deal with the problems facing the church, recommending new approaches, new ways of holding services, new models of church.

'Look at all these books,' she said. 'All of them have good things to say, things that the church needed to hear. But they all started from the wrong end.'

'What do you mean?'

'When your product stops selling, the obvious thing to do is change the advertising, the way it's promoted. Businesses do that all the time, and we tried doing that with church. We introduced modern marketing methods, put adverts in all the right places. That didn't work. No matter what adverts we put up, how many stories we placed in the media, the decline continued. So, we looked again at the business model. Maybe it was the packaging, rather than the advertising. So we tried all kinds of image makeovers.'

She picked up a book, recommending that the church adopt a particular American approach.

'We went through all that as well,' she said. 'Changing the style of our services, doing things differently, playing different music – all well and good. But it didn't address the core problem. You see the problem wasn't the advertising and the problem wasn't the packaging.' She paused.

'The problem was the product,' I concluded. 'No-one wanted the product.'

She nodded. 'Change the advertising if you like, change the packaging, call it by a different name, rebrand it to your heart's content. The real problem with the church by the year 2000 was that no-one wanted the product. Which is kind of ironic, because there was, at that time, a massive interest in spiritual things. You couldn't move in bookshops for books on Taoism, Wicca, Astrology, Patagonian Tree Frog worship – all that mind, body, spirit stuff. What the church failed to realise is that people were searching for spiritual truths; it's just they didn't think they would find them in the church. When it came to spiritual matters, people were full of questions; they just didn't think that the church would have any of the answers.'

'So, you're saying that it wasn't Christianity they rejected, it was the church?'

She nodded. 'Part of it was, I guess, that familiarity had bred a certain amount of contempt. But the real problem was that people looked at the Christians and they couldn't see any difference.' She sighed. 'I remember that some people used to argue that the reason Christianity didn't appeal to a wider audience was that it was too different. But the real reason that we failed to make an impact is that we simply weren't different enough. We rushed around trying to find alternative forms of worship, when we should have been concentrating on finding a truly authentic lifestyle.'

'So we should have been more different,' I said. 'More "noticeable". What do you suggest that we should have done. Wear habits? Shave our heads? Walk around wearing large signs saying "the end is nigh"?'

She looked at me sadly. 'If you're not going to take this seriously you might as well go back now.'

'Sorry.'

'And anyway, you don't need to shave your head.' She smiled, pleased at her joke. 'It's got nothing to do with clothing. Being distinctive is not a question of apparel, but attitude. In fact you might say that was part of the problem. We thought that being distinctive was just a matter of wearing a dog-collar or putting a fish sticker on the bumper of the car. It was precisely because we thought that Christianity was a matter of the external things that we got things so wrong. From Monday to Friday we were just like the society around us. We lived in the same houses, drove the same cars, followed the same adverts, dressed in the same labels, joined the same clubs, held the same prejudices and opinions. The only difference was that on Sunday mornings we went to church and they went to a car boot sale.'

She stared out of the window. 'We got sloppy. We were in the middle of a society that was desperate for someone to show them a better way of life and we let them down. We weren't different. We didn't live in a radical way. Instead we tried to make ourselves more like them. Stupid. That was the point. People in your time didn't want a kind of religious entertainment. They wanted something that made demands, something that challenged, something that was radical, dangerous, thrilling. We should have been living lives that challenged our society, lives that were on the edge. Instead we did everything we could to move a dangerous, disruptive faith back into safer waters. We thought that what was needed was to make Christianity attractive to people, yet if you look at Jesus, if you look at the history of the early church, you discover that what attracted people to

Christianity was that it was *not* attractive. It was wild, dangerous, subversive. And we made it comfortable, cosy and convenient.

'And when they did venture into church they didn't find the answers they were looking for. We wanted to give them things to believe in, but they wanted somewhere to belong. We told them what to think when they needed to be shown how to live. We made them feel guilty when they needed to feel loved.' She stopped and stared at me. 'They came to us for bread,' she said. 'And we handed them a stone.'

She stared at me.

'You have to tell them,' she said. 'You have to tell them that it's not enough to talk about the good news. We have to *be* the good news.'

For a moment, sitting there, sipping tea, on a sunny afternoon in an English village, it seemed like nothing had changed. Then there was a buzzing sound and the front door began to speak.

'Alert, citizen-resident,' it said. 'Your egg-pod is waiting outside.'

'Thank you,' said Lydia.

I looked at her. 'Does your door normally speak to you?'

'Oh yes,' she said. 'I think you'll find that rather a lot of things speak in this day and age. She started to rise from the chair. 'Come on,' she chivvied. 'You've had your tea now. Time to get going. Our cruiser is waiting outside.'

I stood up and walked to the front door, which slid open with a barely perceptible hiss. There outside was a large, transparent, plastic egg, hovering six inches above ground.

And I realised that nothing was the same at all.

Dear Miles,

Well, now we are moving into my territory. I may not know much about 2040, but AD 40 is a period in which I feel at home. Page wrote:

> Yet if you look at Jesus, if you look at the history of the early church, you discover that what attracted people to Christianity was that it was not attractive. It was wild, dangerous, subversive.

I don't much like generalisations of this sort. There were many different churches in the early years of Christianity, just as there were many different communities in which those churches sought to work. Each church had its own problems and its own opportunities; and, in all likelihood, their own way of doing things.

However, I know that you will no doubt accuse me of pedantry. And, at the risk of over-simplification, it is possible to identify common attributes of the early church, certain characteristics which, I venture to say, might help someone like Page in his search for 'authentic' Christianity. After all, if you want 'authenticity', you generally have to go back to the beginning.

Passionate Commitment

Religions thrive and grow through passionate commitment, not through enforced observance. Perhaps the one factor that really identified the early church, and which undoubtedly led to its growth despite the many times of trial and persecution it endured, was that its adherents were passionately committed. They were small, highly committed groups of individuals who were prepared to die for the cause – and who, in many cases, actually *did* die for the cause.

Simple Faith

Faced with a diverse and largely illiterate audience, the early church developed a personal faith that could be simply stated. They created a set of useful, simple, easily memorised statements to remind people what the faith was really about. We can see these in places like 1 Timothy 1:15 ('Christ Jesus came into the world to save sinners') and 4:9 ('we have put our hope in the living God, who is the Saviour of all men, and especially of those who believe') where Paul seems to be quoting from well-known phrases and sayings. In place of the many, often confusing rituals of the Jewish and Pagan world, the early church had simple rituals which took place in a domestic setting.

Collectivist Lifestyle

The early Christians gave up possessions and lived as one family. Private property was surrendered to the community. How long this went on we don't know. It may be that, as time went by and Jesus did not come again, they downgraded this level of commitment. Or it may be that they developed new ways of sharing community. Whatever the case, Christians were known for their sharing, for their strong emphasis on community and for their self-sacrifice.

A Care for the Poor

The early Christians were committed to a practical outworking of their faith, shown through a commitment to the poor, to widows, to outcasts and orphans. They saw this as part and parcel of their faith. Indeed, it wasn't just that they cared for the poor, in many cases they *were* the poor.

Leadership with Equality

The early church appears to have had a simple, 'flat' leadership structure. If we can't be sure about the differences between elders and deacons, we can at least be sure that there is no mention of sub-elders, or deputy-assistant deacons. Even within this simple hierarchy, there was a very strong emphasis on egalitarianism. The Christians were brothers and sisters. Certain people were granted authority, they were still just one part of the body. There was, you will recall, supposed to be no difference between Jew and Gentile, slave and free.

Ethical Purity

The early Christians were diametrically opposed to the world around them. The pagan, Roman world was a world of sex and violence and personal gratification. You couldn't move in most Roman cities without encountering depictions of hardcore, explicit sex. There were paintings on the walls and even on the ceilings. It was also a violent society, where gladiators fought to the death, animals were tortured for sport, and executions were brazenly public. The Christians rejected all this. They rejected the corrupt ethics of the world around them and refused to play a part.

Intimate Involvement

Early churches were small. The earliest dedicated church building dates from around AD 250 – and that was only a converted house. Before that they met in homes, for a worship service that centred around a meal. (The early form of communion had little in common with today's rules and rituals. It took place in the context of a shared meal, and seems to have been open to anyone, as long as their consciences allowed them to take part, or there was no obvious disobedience or sin stopping them.) Equally it was expected that they would all participate in worship. In Paul's discussion of the gifts that can be used for public worship he does not indicate that any of these gifts are confined to any particular gender or social status. Early churches were small, intimate groups with strong social solidarity between the members.

A Sense of Significance

Despite their small size, despite their domestic setting, they obviously took their worship very seriously. This was not a mere social get-together, but *church*, and believers were encouraged to view their gatherings with profound significance. They didn't have a temple, for they themselves were the temple; they didn't have priests, for they were all priests. What they did mattered. Indeed, so significant was their activity that it was, for many, literally a matter of life and death.

If Page is calling for a church which is truly distinctive and counter-culture then he could do worse than take a long look at where the whole thing started. Simple faith, collectivist lifestyle, a care for the poor, leadership and equality, ethical purity, intimate involvement, passionate commitment and a deep sense of significance. How many of those qualities are present in today's UK church? Instead, we have a vast array of rules and regulations and huge, unwieldy hierarchies; we have a church that is wealthy and surburban; we have a church that, far from being set apart from the world around it, often plays exactly the same games and indulges in exactly the same kind of vices. And we have a church which, even to its adherents, doesn't seem to matter anymore.

In its early days, Christianity was a counter-culture, subversive operation. Now, it's just part of the establishment.

––––––––––––

So much for the early church. Looking back at what I have just written, I am surprised at my vehemence. For so long the UK church has been a matter of indifference to me – or of purely academic interest. Perhaps I care more about it than I suspected!

It is all this thinking that you are getting me doing. In fact, I do think this exercise is doing me some good. It struck me that, just as in my last letter I accused the church of holding on to the past and not letting go, I was doing precisely the same thing. So, last night, I took a deep breath and started to clear out Caroline's study.

I can't say it was easy. But it was a start.

Give my love to Susan and the children.

Ever yours,
Stephen

tHe liViNg Museum

3

It was 2040.

I was sitting in a large egg.

I had been dead for nine years.

No wonder I had a headache.

'Are you all right?' Lydia asked.

The large, egg-shaped object was moving steadily along, hovering around six inches above the ground. Every now and then it would hit a slight bump, and a computerised voice would gently chirrup, 'Sorry.' Our seats were plush and red and soft. The air inside the egg was warm and in the background some soothing music was playing. It was like driving along in a turbocharged womb.

'Are you okay?' asked Lydia again.

'I'm okay,' I said. 'Just having a bit of a struggle taking it all in.' Through the semi-transparent walls of the egg I could see the fields and houses flash by. Some houses were just as I recalled them, others were strange and new; angular, stark creations, gleaming with chrome and light. 'Where are we going?' I asked.

'We're going to church,' Lydia replied. 'In fact, we're going to the Cathedral.'

'Typical!' I exclaimed. 'That's still going. Typical! No matter what happens the establishment survives. You could explode a nuclear bomb in London, but it's a fair bet that the Sunday after some old bloke would be standing there in his vestments doing the same old thing ...'

She looked at me coolly. 'You know, Nick,' she said, 'you're not here to condemn but to learn. At least try to keep an open mind. Just for once in your life.'

Before I could issue a suitably crushing reply, the egg-cruiser had swerved round a corner, and I realised that we were coming into Oxford. There were the familiar gleaming spires. There were the pale, butter-coloured Cotswold stone buildings, their jagged edges smoothed by time. Admittedly there were some differences, notably in that many of the colleges seemed to have found new sources of revenue. We passed Nuffield College, which had a large sign saying 'Sponsored by Yamakuzi Autos, Makers of the Morris Oxford Egg-Cruiser'. We passed Brasenose College, now sponsored by 'Vick's Inhaler'. And Worcester College, now apparently sponsored by 'Lea and Perrins'.

I had little time to take this all in, however, before the egg slowed gently to a halt. A door hissed open. Outside, there was the old front gate of Christchurch College, massive and imposing, looking much as it did forty years ago; indeed, much as it had looked four hundred years ago. We walked through the front gate and crossed the quad towards the double arched entrance to the Cathedral. Over the arches was a large sign.

Welcome to Christchurch Cathedral.
Oxford's Living Museum of Christianity

'Good joke,' I said. 'Good to see that the students still have a sense of humour. Is this something to do with rag week?'

Lydia sighed. 'This is the future, remember? Just because you have overactive sense-of-humour glands, doesn't mean that everything around you is a joke. This sign is for real.'

'For real? You mean it's really a ...'

'A museum,' she nodded. 'Yes.'

I looked again at the sign. A 'living museum'. It conjured up images of attractions I had taken my children to see – castles and farms and industrial-age villages where all the staff dressed in traditional costumes, trying to conjure up the past, to recreate a reality that had disappeared long, long ago.

'Come on,' said Lydia. 'Let's go in.'

Inside the Cathedral things looked much as they had always looked. The stained glass glowed softly in the sunlight, the stones beneath our feet echoed with history. There was even a vicar standing there to welcome us. His head was crowned with what appeared to be an ill-fitting grey wig and he was wearing a pair of small, half-moon glasses of the type that went out of fashion in about 1927. But what was noticeable about him was that he was wearing the full garb. Black cassock, white surplice, and various other bits which may have possibly included an alb. Or perhaps a chasuble. I never could tell the difference.

'Hello, my child,' he said, and he made the sign of the cross.

I looked around.

'Is he talking to me?' I whispered to Lydia.

'It's all part of the show,' she said.

'Welcome to the Cathedral, my son' he continued. 'Here you will find everything done exactly as it was in the past. May I give you this replica church notice sheet? It will help to explain things. You see that we will be staging a choral evensong reconstruction at 1800 hours, or if you prefer a more "interactive" experience, you can join in with our virtual choir rehearsal at 1330. Of course, if you really want to immerse yourself in the full traditional church experience, there's a PCC meeting at 1500 hours where members of the museum staff will be restaging an argument about the pews.'

I stared at him. 'Where did you do your research for this part?' I asked. 'Old sitcoms was it? Or films from the nineteen forties?'

He smiled. 'I can assure you that we have all been trained to give our visitors a fully authentic ecclesiastical experience. My costume is historically accurate to the last degree.'

I looked at him critically. 'Your costume might be accurate,' I said, 'But it's the character that's all wrong. You're not a real vicar. You're too bright and shiny. You don't have that "hunted" look . . .'

He smiled smoothly. 'Well, Citizen, I think the experts know best, don't you?'

'Know best?' I snarled. Something about him started to make my blood boil. It was the fakery, the gaudiness, the sheer effrontery of it all. 'They don't know anything. The vicars I know are good men, honest men,' I snarled. 'They deserve better than to be counterfeited by some out-of-work actor with fake hair and a nice line in costume.'

He looked offended. 'I'm sorry, my son . . .' he began.

'And don't call me "son",' I added. 'You might be wearing a dress but that doesn't make you my mother. I'm old enough to be your grandfather . . .'

The 'vicar' stopped looking holy for a moment. In fact an expression of what might be termed 'menace' entered his eyes.

'Now you listen to me . . . ,' he said. 'This museum is a tribute to the golden age of church-going. And we don't take kindly to anyone who tarnishes the memory. Geddit?'

Lydia pulled my arm.

'Don't mind him,' she said to the museum attendant, 'he's not very well. He's got a bit of a problem.'

The 'vicar' looked at me, took a step back and turned his menace down a notch.

'Yes, well, tell him to take it easy,' he said. 'We don't want him spoiling the fun for everyone else.'

'Spoiling the fun?' I hissed. 'Of course I'm going to spoil the fun. I'm a Christian. That's what we do best!'

Lydia started to drag me away.

'He's mad,' said the 'vicar'. 'You ought to have him scanned.'

'Yes,' she said. 'Thanks for your understanding.'

'I'm dead you know!' I called over my shoulder as Lydia pulled me into a corner, 'Like this place!'

Lydia sat me down in what was labelled as 'an authentic church plastic chair. c.1972'.

'Look,' she said. 'Let's get one thing straight at the start. You have to take things calmly. You can't charge around insulting people. It won't help to get angry.'

'But look at it! Nothing left but a meaningless, fake, tourist attraction.' I paused. 'I mean, I know in my day it was often meaningless. And a tourist attraction. But at least it wasn't fake.' There was a long pause. 'Well, not always . . . ,' I said.

Lydia smiled. 'Perhaps I rushed you here too quickly,' she said. 'Maybe I should have given you more time to adjust to things . . .' Then she shook her head. 'No,' she said. 'We just don't have the time.' She turned to me. 'Just try to understand, Nick, that you're here to learn. You can have a heart attack back in your own century, if you like, but here and now, you need to keep calm and keep looking around.'

I nodded. 'Okay,' I said. 'I'll try.'

She smiled. 'Just have a look around.'

I followed her advice and started to wander around the Cathedral to look at the exhibits. It was obvious, from the way things were set out and labelled and displayed, that this was no longer a living church. It was a learning centre, an archive, a monument. It had been stuffed and mounted. It was clear that if people wanted to find out about Christianity in 2040, they had to visit a museum.

I stopped at one table on which was a display of old prayer-books. Suddenly, the table spoke to me.

'Hello Visitor,' it said. 'And welcome to Display Table Number Four. Would you like me to explain about prayerbooks?'

I looked uncertainly at the table.

'Er . . . are you talking to me?'

'Of course, Visitor. I am fully programmed to explain these artefacts for your information.'

'Oh. Thank you very much. I . . . er . . . I'm just not used to talking furniture, that's all.'

There was a pause. 'Visitor is not used to talking furniture,' muttered the table. 'Ah. I see. No, Visitor, I am not furniture, I am Learniture.'

'Learniture?'

'Yes!' chirruped the table proudly. 'Furniture that helps you learn. Obviously the Visitor is from some incredibly primitive country that does not have Learniture yet, or else Visitor has just woken from a very deep coma and did not know that Learniture was introduced twelve years ago by the Yakamumu-Ikea Corporation of Japan. Or else Visitor is just very, very slow on the uptake.'

I tried to remember what Lydia had said to me about remaining calm.

'I think it might be a combination of all those,' I said. 'Please do go on.'

The table gave a satisfied 'hmph' and cleared its throat. (Or whatever it is that a talking table clears.) 'Well,' it began, 'let me tell you about the Prayer Book. The original Anglican prayer book was devised in the sixteenth century as a means of standardising the services and theology of the Anglican Church. It remained largely unchanged until the late twentieth century when the church suddenly realised that no-one understood it anymore. It then went through several revisions: The Alternative Service Book was the first, then we had Common Worship in 2000, Very Common Worship in 2009 and Downright Rude Worship in 2015 . . .'

'I'm sorry?'

The box hiccoughed. 'Just my little joke,' it said. 'I have highly developed humour circuitry.'

'You could have fooled me.'

'Oh,' said the table, huffily, 'you're *that* kind of visitor.' It gave a kind of metallic sniff. 'Anyway, it underwent many revisions, all of which had two things in common: first they took a huge amount of time, energy, and theological debate. Second, no-one understood them any better than the first one. Still, it made them feel like they were trying. In places like this, the older, seventeenth century form was generally used, with services such as Matins, Evensong, and sung Eucharist. It is those traditions that we keep alive in this museum today. Now, Visitor, if you would like to make your way to Table Four, you can see a collection of late twentieth century parish magazines . . .'

I shook my head sadly and turned away.

The Cathedral was full of signs and displays, of carefully recreated 'exhibits' demonstrating what Christian worship used to be like.

You could be photographed in traditional clerical dress (Vicar €25, Bishop €40 and Archbishop €60). You could try your hand at bell-ringing. You could blend your own incense and swing it around in a censer. It was the whole interactive experience.

Everything was there except sincerity. Everything except the real thing.

'Doesn't anyone worship here any more?' I asked.

'Oh yes,' replied Lydia. 'They worship what many of them have always worshipped: the past.'

I nodded. 'You're right. That was the problem with the traditionalists. They wanted the church pickled and preserved in a jar. Keep the old ways, don't change a thing, keep wearing the costume and chanting the chants. While all around, the world outside changes.' I looked around. 'These places always were museums,' I said. 'The only difference now is that they've put up the signs.'

Lydia was quiet.

'There may be something in what you say,' she said at last. 'But even so, I'm not sure you ever really understood their point of view.' We began to walk up the north aisle. 'You always went on and on about relevance and "contemporary meaning", but maybe you forgot the importance of tradition. Tradition was important to people, far more important, in fact, than many evangelical and more trendy churches ever understood.' She turned and pointed to a notice board, on which was a list of services with dates and times.

'To follow a pattern of services, a familiar routine of worship, gives people a rhythm to their life,' she said. 'And as people's lives began to fragment at the end of the last century that kind of thing became quite important. Increasingly our work and social lives had no fixed points, nothing to anchor them or hold them steady. Church services, with their traditional patterns and rhythms had always provided a structure for people's lives, something solid and familiar and strong. Built into the stones of the parish church and woven into the history of the villages and towns.'

'But they had to offer more than that,' I said. 'I mean, church had to be more than a set of village traditions.'

'Of course. And where the traditionalists went wrong is that they thought that merely holding on to these things was enough. That repetition was a virtue in and of itself. But you have to keep working at these things, you have to keep explaining the significance and reminding people of the history. Traditions become meaningless when no-one explains them. At their best traditional forms of worship ground people in the history of their faith, reinforcing the sense of permanence, of meaning. Those participating were following in the footsteps of millions of others over thousands of years. Some people found that more comforting and meaningful than the twenty-first century's endless addiction to novelty.'

I nodded. We were standing in front of the great stained glass window at one end of the Cathedral. The sun was setting and the evening light through the window painted us all in red and blue and gold.

'And the other thing they gave us was beauty. Traditional forms of worship appealed to the aesthetic sense in people. Say what you like about them, they looked and sounded beautiful.'

I nodded, thinking of the last time I had been in this Cathedral. A sung Eucharist on a spring evening. Beautiful singing, rich language. An unmistakable sense of peace and reflection.

'Of course, more trendy churches scoffed at this, but let's face it, what did they have to offer along those lines? What, we may ask, was the artistic high point of the evangelical church? The banner. Hardly surprising that people who were looking for art, for beauty, for something a bit deeper, were left feeling unfulfilled.'

'So what are you saying?' I countered. 'That we should all get our vestments on again? That we should go back to all this?'

'No,' she replied. 'I'm simply saying that art is important. Beauty is important. You, above all, should appreciate that. You were a writer after all.'

'Thank you for remembering . . .'

'Of course all your stuff is out of print now,' she continued, 'but the point is still valid. Still, never mind that. The traditional liturgy had beautiful language, the music had been created by great artists. It had a quality that was entirely different. For some people that was important.'

'Yes, I understand that. But if it was so great then why were the high churches, the "liturgical" churches dying out in my time?'

She sighed. 'Like with tradition, it's not enough just to have beauty. You have to have understanding. Traditionalism appeals to a certain sort of people,' Lydia continued. 'And that's fine. But it's important for them to know what it is they are responding to. It's not enough just to like the music or the images or the richness of the language. You have to understand what it's all about. You have to bring it into reality in your life. What we forget about the 1662 service was that, in 1662 people knew what it meant. But the further you get from the original time, the more remote the language is. In the end the words sound beautiful, but no meaning is left.

'That's why traditionalism led so often to nominal Christianity. People went along to the services because they loved the style, but they never really understood the message. It became an aesthetic experience, a part of their routine, but not a reality.'

'It became a living museum,' I said. She nodded.

'Christianity isn't experience alone, but fact and knowledge as well. Too often what happened with traditional churches was that they kept the traditions alive, but the faith died.'

'Surely many other churches did the same,' I countered. 'They just had different traditions and experiences . . .'

'Of course. Baptist, Methodist, house churches went the same way. Every church where the form of what they were doing became more important than the content. Modern "worship times" were just as vulnerable to that trap.' She looked around her. 'It's just much more visible here. That's why we came here first. Because this is the biggest symbol of all that we have lost. There was a time when what went on in here *meant* something. When the language really spoke to people, when the beauty and mystery were a part of everyday reality as well. But we became complacent. We forgot that language changes, that people change. We carried on doing beautiful services, but forgot to tell people why.'

She turned towards me.

'Learn what you can. The church of your time rightly rejected the nominalism, the archaism, the general lack of understanding. What it didn't do was incorporate the depth, the richness, the artistry. It didn't become a regular part of people's lives. And it too assumed that people understood the language and forms it was using. It made, in its own way, the same mistake.'

As we went outside again I said to Lydia, 'Are there no "traditional" churches left?'

'Hardly any. The Anglican Church tore itself apart in a series of squabbles. Women priests, homosexuality, forms of worship, a defender of faith who talked to his plants, the canonisation of David Beckham –'

'The *what*?'

'It's too complicated to go into now. But in a way, all those things were just symptoms. The real problem with the established church was structural. The structure meant that, when the hard times came, it just couldn't cope. It used to pride itself on being a broad church, but a broad church can only be held together by a strong, widely accepted leadership. In the twenty-first century nobody believed in that kind of leadership anymore. Take the central leadership away and all the parts just drifted off in different directions.'

We left the 'Living Museum', bidding a farewell to the fake vicar, who gave us a cheery sign of the cross. Outside, in the setting sun, the Cotswold stone of the Oxford college glowed softly yellow. I turned to look back at the entrance to the Cathedral and noticed that, alone among the buildings, it was shrouded in shadow.

Dear Miles,

This latest episode raises a good many questions.

I suppose the first one that occurred to me centres around the very idea that formed the basis of this 'museum'; the idea that there was, as the character in the museum says 'a golden age of church-going' . . . a time when we lived in 'Christian Britain'.

Of course, it all depends on what you mean by 'Christian'. If you mean a Britain which had a fairly well-accepted Christian culture, then this might be true. But if you mean a country which acted in a 'Christian' way then I'm not sure that that is the case. The peak year for church attendance was probably 1904; ever since then, the church has been in decline. But if 1904 was the high-point of Christian influence in Britain, it doesn't say much for the zealousness of their faith. In 1904 we as a society were still engaged in the unjust, evil business of empire. We were still locking up children. The working class were living in appalling slum-filled conditions. There were, admittedly, far more people in churches, but these were the same churches which had special pews for the Lord of the Manor or the Squire, with everyone else renting whatever pew they could afford. (I should be interested to know what kind of sermon the vicars of these churches could have preached on the book of James.) There was a time when the churches were full of people; but that doesn't mean that they all believed it or lived it.

Personally, I think it is time the church gave up the illusion of a golden age. It is difficult to march forward with any kind of conviction if you are always looking back over your shoulder.

The second issue I want to address rises out of another aspect of the heritage of British Christianity, but this time in a more practical way. I mean all those ancient churches. The Anglican Church has probably the most expensive, labour-intensive buildings of any organisation in the country, with the possible exception of the aristocracy and the Oxbridge universities. Many congregations meet in listed buildings, buildings which they can't afford to run and which are no longer suitable for their worship, even if they could afford them. If you were starting an organisation with only a small group of committed supporters, would you choose to house them all in listed buildings?

One can't help but feel that the relationship between many congregations and their church buildings is neither helpful, nor, indeed, very healthy. There is a tremendous emotional attachment to the building itself, the symbol of the church's once powerful presence. The buildings become like a demanding, elderly relative. Of course we're all still fond of Auntie; it's just if we'd be far better off if we could pop her into a home and let someone else take care of her.

It's not even as if the church can afford the buildings any more. As church attendance declines, so does the church bank balance. Dioceses are in deep financial problems. The church commissioners have seen hundreds of millions wiped off their assets through a mixture of stock market downturns and sheer old-fashioned incompetence. Several dioceses are close to bankruptcy. In Scotland, the Episcopal Church's pension fund has a £50m deficit because of the stock market downturn, while the Church of Scotland's website even has a page listing properties for sale. (When I last looked you could snap up a redundant church for around £100,000).

So this is not a good time to be lumbered with hugely expensive, high maintenance, historically significant buildings. The fact is that the church – and here we are mainly talking about the Church of England – owns a huge number of listed buildings which it cannot possibly afford. And, talking to friends of mine who still tread the corridors of power in the Anglican Church (wherever those corridors are), there is an unspoken fear that someday English Heritage will get a law passed making it compulsory for the owners to maintain listed buildings.

It seems to me that you, as a card-carrying member of the Anglican Church, ought to be pushing your lords and masters to develop a strategy to deal with the cumbersome heritage of the church before it is too late. Otherwise we face the real possibility that either hundreds of listed buildings will have to be pulled down; or the church will be forced by law to divert precious funds to maintain buildings it no longer wants but can't get rid of.

For nonconformist churches the solutions are sometimes more straightforward, since it is rarer for them to be lumbered with an ancient building. Many churches have sold the land to developers and used the fund to build a smaller, more flexible building or to build up funds for workers.

Of course, many people are unwilling to think realistically about the future of their building because it is seen as an admission of defeat.

What the church has to learn – and it would do well to learn it before it has the lesson forcibly applied – is how to close things down. This might mean transferring ownership of historic buildings to organisations who are better equipped to care for them; it might even mean helping terminally ill congregations to a peaceful end.

It would definitely mean returning to the early church model of meeting in houses. There is no evidence of a church building until about the third century. Before that, their 'sacred spaces' where simply people's homes. Easy to maintain, flexible, low-cost accommodation. That, I suspect is the future, whether we like it or not. I can't imagine that God would prefer his people to spend their time patching up old buildings when they could be creating new lives.

Finally, I think we need to take care when analysing Page's comments about beauty. I don't disagree with him, but too often we confuse 'beautiful' with 'ornate'.

Have I ever spoken to you about 'wabi-sabi'? It is a Japanese concept which I find quite attractive. Wabi-sabi means the beauty of simple things, of things imperfect and humble. As one writer defines it: 'Wabi-sabi is a beauty of things imperfect, impermanent, and incomplete. It is the beauty of things modest and humble. It is the beauty of things unconventional.'

This, it seems to me, is what is missing from so much worship today. If there is art and beauty then it is often complicated. A Bach chorale, ornate, gilded vestments; a stained glass window – all these are undeniably beautiful; but so is the intricate tracery of a leaf; so is a plain white wall; so is a simple wooden table and chair. So is a cross.

What matters is the deliberate act of looking; the conscious desire to see beauty as a way of worshipping God. Beauty can be found in bread and wine and in silence and reflection. In liturgy too, as Page says, as long as that liturgy is not complex and difficult to navigate. The last time I went to evensong at a Cathedral I got completely lost. Liturgy brings us a sense of the mysterious. But it is one thing to have a sense of mystery; it is another thing entirely to mystify everyone.

I suppose what I am trying to say is that an emphasis on the aesthetic senses does not mean a lot of complicated art, but that the visual, the physical, and the reflective should be integrated into our worship as much as the cerebral and intellectual.

I should like to see some wabi-sabi worship; modest, humble, unconventional. It would take place in wabi-sabi buildings; simple, domestic, ordinary. And it would reflect, perhaps, a wabi-sabi God; a God who delights in things imperfect, impermanent and incomplete, and who wants to bring to them permanence, perfection and completeness.

Ever yours,
Stephen

tHe aRchBishoP

From the centre of Oxford, the egg-shaped pod hummed briefly south. As we crossed over the river it seemed that little had changed; the sinuous curve of the water, the dappled shadows of the trees, students punting, a young woman and a hairy old man sculling gently upstream, deep in conversation.

Beyond the river there were more significant changes. Eggs hummed by, floating across the ground in quiet efficiency. Most of the houses were the same as forty years ago, but beyond them and between there were glimpses of new buildings, built of chrome and steel and sheets of glass as dark and mysterious as a mountain pool.

After a few minutes the egg drew gently to a stop and the door slid open with its quiet hiss.

We were on the outskirts of the city. Opposite us was an ancient church which, like the church in my village, now appeared to be some form of residence. Either that or the congregation had decided to add a conservatory to the south aisle and dig a swimming pool in the graveyard.

I pointed to it. 'How did they get permission to do that?' I asked. 'Surely the churches are protected as they were in my time?'

'Oh no,' said Lydia. 'All that went years ago. As the congregations dwindled, it became economically impossible for them to maintain the buildings. The government tried to force legislation onto the churches, but there was simply no money. The congregations just locked the doors and went elsewhere. So, in the end the government had to face that either they would have to maintain all these buildings, or they would have to let the buildings take their chances in the open market. Which is precisely what happened.' She pointed to the building. 'That one went fifteen years ago. Funnily enough it's owned by the chairman of the company who were responsible for your ... well ... your unfortunate "accident".'

'Yes, I've been meaning to talk to you about that ...,' I said.

'Haven't got time now,' said Lydia, rather too hurriedly for my liking. 'Anyway – we're not going there, we're going over the road.'

We crossed the narrow lane from the old church and passed by a large red-brick building. Although some new buildings had sprung up around it, and although there were huge, misty-coloured glass windows and what looked like a massive, circular solar panel on the roof, I recognised it.

'This is the diocesan headquarters, isn't it?' I asked. 'Church House.'

'*Was,*' replied Lydia. 'It *was* the headquarters.'

'You mean they've moved?'

'Well, not so much moved as dissolved,' she replied. 'I suppose technically there is still a diocese,' she said. 'I mean no-one's ever disbanded it, but it's all a bit meaningless now. How can you have a diocese if there are no churches in it?'

I looked up at the big building. On the side, I could just make out a pattern of light-coloured bricks which had once formed the shape of a cross; now the shape was mostly covered by a huge sign saying 'Panergistic Management Inc. – Radical Organisational Solutions for Today's World'.

'What about all the people who used to work here?' I asked. 'Are they all gone? Has all the hierarchy disappeared? You know, what about all those bishops and Archbishops? I can't believe they've all given up.'

'No, not all of them,' Lydia replied. 'The Archbishop of Canterbury is still around.'

'I thought so,' I said, smugly. 'I'll bet he's still living in Lambeth Palace.'

'Not exactly,' she said. She pointed across the road to a small, nondescript, semi-detached house. 'In fact he lives over there. Shall we go and visit?'

→•←

We knocked at a green painted door, and after a few moments, it was opened by a small, elderly man dressed in a tatty old pair of jeans and what looked like some kind of silver cardigan, which pulsated with light. Under the high-tech exterior, however, I could see the age-old uniform of a dog collar and clerical shirt. He looked at us quizzically.

'Is the Archbishop in?' I asked.

He smiled. 'Of course,' he replied. 'You are expected.' He peered past me. 'Hello, Lydia.'

'Hi,' said Lydia. 'I'll leave him to you, shall I?'

'You're not coming in to meet the Archbishop?' I asked.

'No. I've got some errands to do. See you later.' She turned and left and the old man shut the door.

After passing down a dimly lit hall I was led into a sitting room and offered a large, plastic armchair to sit in. As I sat in the chair, it seemed to respond to my body, moulding itself to suit me. The old man left the room for a moment and I could hear him pottering around in the kitchen. Then he returned with a tray of tea and biscuits which he put on the table by my chair.

He then turned and, instead of going to fetch the Archbishop, sat down in the chair opposite me.

'Er ... Aren't you going to fetch the Archbishop?' I asked.

He smiled. 'I *am* the Archbishop,' he replied. 'Do help yourself to the Custard Creams.'

'I'm terribly sorry,' I stammered. 'I was expecting something ... er ... different.'

'Oh, please, don't apologise,' said the Archbishop. 'I quite understand. You were expecting pomp and ceremony and assistants running around and all that kind of stuff.'

'Well, yes,' I replied, thinking of the only time I had met the Archbishop, when he was accompanied by a press officer and several other officials.

'No, we don't have any of that any more,' said the Archbishop. He pressed a small remote control and the teapot began to automatically pour the tea. 'It's more of an honorary title nowadays, you know,' he said. 'A bit like the Sheriff of Nottingham or the Warden of the Cinque Ports. We share it about among ourselves. It's my turn this year. Next year I think it's going to be Doris's go.'

'Doris?' I asked.

'The Bishop of Liverpool,' he replied. 'Nice lady. Still runs a church.'

I slowly digested this information. It seemed a cruel irony that, just as a woman Archbishop finally came along, all the churches had disappeared.

'Well,' I said. 'At least it's nice to hear that there are still some churches about.'

'Churches? Of course there are still some churches!' he exclaimed. He looked shocked. 'There were thirty-seven at the last count.'

There was a pause.

'Thirty-seven,' I said. 'Er ... that's not very many, is it?'

'We are not,' he said, absent-mindedly stirring his tea with his pencil, 'as big a denomination as we once were.'

Calling this an understatement was an understatement. 'You're hardly a denomination at all,' I said. 'More like a very spread-out house group.'

'Well, we still keep the structures going,' said the Archbishop, with a sigh, 'albeit in a scaled-down size. We had a very successful General Synod last month, in the back room of the "Rose and Crown" in Tooting. And of course, worldwide the Anglican Church is still going strong. It's just here that ... well, the last forty years have not been kind to us.' He sipped his tea. 'It's a bit like the English and football, really. We invented it, but everyone else seems to do it better than us.'

'But what happened?' I asked. 'Where did we go so wrong?'

He looked at me, and for the first time there was real sadness in his eyes.

'I think it was in the reign of Queen Victoria,' he said.

The Archbishop gazed into the distance for a moment, absent-mindedly dipping his tie in his tea. He suddenly noticed what he was doing, pulled the tie out quickly and sucked the tea off it.

'You see, most of our church structures belong to a different age,' he continued, 'an age of hierarchy and order; an age of rigid class distinction, where everyone knew their place and listened to their elders and betters. It was a system that served for centuries. And then something happened: society changed. People began to distrust authority. The second half of the twentieth century was marked by individualism, in people asserting their rights and rebelling against authority. In the workplace, there were moves towards different kinds of management structure and demands for more personal involvement in decision making. Vast, cumbersome bureaucratic organisations were replaced by flexible, leaner, more responsive structures. More and more decision making was pushed downward, giving people more control over their lives at a local level.'

He sighed.

'For the churches, this proved a problem. Some of the nonconformist denominations could react more quickly. The Baptists had always had a large degree of autonomy in their churches and many of the independent churches had their own, virtually new management structures. For many of the others, however, such change was virtually impossible.' He smiled.

'So how did you respond to these changes? What happened?'

He shook his head. 'Nothing,' he said. 'Nothing happened. What's more it happened slowly. The denominations had become bureaucracies – and in a bureaucracy it is more important that everyone perform to the same level than that some excel. So people were appointed to senior posts because of their loyalty or their political skills, or because they had spent their career playing by the rules. Rarely were appointments made because the person involved had a track record in leading churches to growth. We needed people who could think in new ways, do new things, but the structure of our organisations was not built to enable new things to happen; it was built to keep things exactly the same as they had always been.'

He smiled sadly, lost for a moment in his thoughts.

'I used to go to General Synods or denominational conferences,' he said, 'and look around me and wonder where the young people were. And then I realised that they all had better things to do.'

I sipped my tea. It tasted of plastic.

'Maybe,' I said, 'the problem was not only with the structures but with the very idea of denominations. I mean, I went to a Baptist church for most of my life and then became an Anglican without hardly noticing it. It simply wasn't an issue for me. They seemed to be the same kind of Christians as me.'

He looked at me quizzically. 'You remember the denominations? You don't look old enough,' he said.

'I'm young for my age.'

He shrugged. 'Well, of course, you are right. Fewer people bothered about whether they went to an Anglican or a Baptist church, only whether their church was alive or dead. But even so, we did nothing to diminish the sense that we were irrelevant. We still put out this air of being too much part of the establishment.'

'Well, you *were* part of the establishment.'

'I know, and didn't it cause us all kind of problems? You know that in the established church there were a great many radical thinkers. A great many truly holy men and women, people who were dedicated to serving their Lord, who gave everything they had in the service of some of the most desperate people in the land. But whenever people thought of "the Church" they thought of an extension of the government. Or possibly a sort of cousin to the monarchy. They thought of dog collars and royal weddings and men in dresses sitting in the House of Lords. Everyone knew it couldn't last, but we should have been braver. We should have severed the link between the church and the state in order to strengthen the link between the church and the people.'

'So what could you have done differently?'

'We should have marketed ourselves a lot better for a start,' he said, with sudden energy. 'As I said, it's not as if we weren't doing good things. There were urban initiatives, training schemes, mission programmes. And despite the faults of the parish system, it at least kept churches in the inner cities. We kept working in there when all the bigger, newer, trendier, "successful" churches moved out to the suburbs.' He paused. 'But we weren't any good at telling people about it or challenging them to be involved. What the Anglican Church, in particular, needed at the beginning of the new millennium was a complete shake-up, a total restructuring of the way the denomination worked.' He shrugged. 'Didn't get it, of course. There were too many people in there who liked the whole archaic system with its chain of command and its career structure and the endless committees and debates.'

He lifted his hands in exasperation as if the struggle were still going on in front of him. 'We should have learned from the businesses!' he suddenly exclaimed. 'Decentralise. Give authority to those who can use it best. Above all, resource the churches. We should have concentrated on providing them with the right tools to do the job.'

'You mean money?'

'I mean people.' He looked at me steadily. 'All organisational structures find their natural expression in people. Dynamic, exciting structures are populated by dynamic, exciting workers. Tired, old structures are too often staffed by tired, old people. And that's how it went on. We provided the churches with leaders who were too content to operate within the old structures, indeed, who were products of the old structures. Leaders who could talk but not listen. Leaders who were trained to be everything to everybody and in the end became nothing very much to nobody in particular. Ministers and pastors who were forced to keep the old, crumbling structures going and who, in the end, tended to disappear up their own committees. They had been trained in the classical model, where they were in charge of the church by virtue of the position they held, but what was needed were real leaders – people who could develop gifts, spot potential and build networks; leaders who could lead by example rather than by appointment. Leaders who could create their own accountability structures at a local level. Because it was no good looking for management or accountability to rural deans or canons or bishops or area superintendents. Those days were gone.'

He paused.

'I'll show you something,' he said. He reached across to a large box of some sort of lightweight plastic. He opened the box and took out, from layers of soft padding, a gorgeous, glowing bishop's mitre. It was gold and silver and decorated with crimson flames which, in that dark room seemed to glow and flicker with light, so that it appeared to me not like a hat but as a kind of lamp, a beacon on a hillside, a flame in the darkness.

'There was a time,' he said, 'when wearing this *meant* something. When the people listened to what the wearer had to say. But we took their attention for granted, and we thought more about the hat than the person who wore it.' He paused and smiled. 'It would be nice to wear it again. But nowadays, I fear, it would be little more than fancy dress.'

He cradled the mitre in his arms and, for the first time, he seemed what he was; a tired, shattered old man. And, as night fell, we sat there in silence, while he held a symbol that no-one understood any more, and I looked on a lamp where the light was slowly going out.

Dear Miles,

In thinking about this manuscript, and in researching its claims, I have been trying to formulate a reason why some denominations can respond quicker than others to crises.

And, as in so many areas of life, it all comes down to management structures.

Here is my theory: denominations fall into two main kinds of management structure: Federal or Imperial.

The Imperial model is the older one. It started when the church became the official church of the Roman Empire, and it follows, broadly speaking, the same Imperial lines. At the top you have an 'emperor', and below him, lots of different levels of authority and responsibility. It is the model used by the Catholic, Orthodox and Anglican Churches; an historical model, which reflects the power structures of a different age. (It is not exclusively restricted to older denominations, however; there are many big 'new' churches which are run on Imperial lines, where the pastor is the emperor and everyone follows his commands.)

The Federal model is different, and was born much more recently – mainly from the late seventeenth century onwards (from, in fact, the time when society itself was developing democratic structures). In the Federal model, individual churches have a large measure of autonomy and control. They can decide on their own direction and activities, appoint their own leaders, etc. However, they are part of a loose federation, a network which also offers some control and guidance. That federation might be a denomination like the Baptists, or it might be a looser collection of churches, such as is found in the Pioneer churches and similar new networks.

Both models have their strengths and weaknesses. The main strength of the Imperial model is that there is someone in charge. There is a figurehead, a leader, whether he be the Pope, the Archbishop of Canterbury or the Patriarch of Alexandria. He (and it always has been a 'he') can set the agenda through his leadership. The main weaknesses of this model are that it is slow to react to circumstances, and that it assumes everyone at the bottom takes any notice of the person at the top. This might have worked in the Middle Ages; it doesn't work so well today.

The strength of the Federal model is that it allows churches much more control over their own destinies. They can react to the needs of their local area, they can define their own forms of worship, they can, within fairly broad parameters, do exactly as they want. Which is also, in my opinion, its main weakness. Because there is no ultimate authority you cannot ask the church to pursue a course it does not want to. Which is why you don't see many of the newer, growing, Federal churches in the inner city. The Anglicans and Catholics are there because the system says they have to be there; the Federal churches can go where they like. So they do.

However, I would have to say that, out of the two models, the Federal model does at least relate more to how people live their lives today. Most people work in businesses which are more Federal than Imperial. They live in a parliamentary democracy; they expect to have a say in the running of their lives. Which is precisely why the Imperial churches have been experimenting with federation. The

Anglican Church, with its PCCs and synods, has been trying to push the authority down. Many congregations have taken effective control of their churches. However the main structure is still Imperial.

Both structures also suffer from the subtle addiction to power. In the Imperial models, power lies in being appointed to certain posts; in the Federal model, power means being elected onto various committees.

In the end, whether a church is run as an empire or as a federation, results are what matters. If the structure is not enabling growth, then it must be changed. The process must be re-engineered. Committees should not outlive their usefulness. Bureaucracy should be kept to a minimum.

Above all, the structures should be transparent. People in our churches don't mind being governed and organised, but they want to know how it is being done. It is ridiculous that no-one in the pews in the C of E understands how the Archbishop of Canterbury is appointed. And the fact is that, unless steps are taken to simplify the structures and to make them transparent, they will not be funded from the congregations. The congregations will set up their own structures, which are closer to their own ideals and towards which they will devote their funding.

This, of course, is not helped by the idea of establishment. You are quite right that I am opposed to this. Indeed, my belief is that the moment in AD 312 when Christianity became the official Roman religion was the darkest day in the history of the church.

Just think what has followed from all that: oppression, corruption, the Crusades, witch hunts, the whole ridiculous panoply of state religion, and now, in our own very recent times, the identification of Christianity with Western Politics.

I know that you do not necessarily agree with me on this one, but regardless of our own differences, I do think this whole establishment issue is one reason why so many people do not look to our churches for answers. (It's also a reason why there is so much complacency about the statistics. 'For heaven's sake,' the official church says, 'how can the church die out? It's protected by law. It's the official sponsor. It's part of the establishment.')

What does establishment mean? We know what it meant: it meant that the Anglican Church was protected and promoted to the exclusion of others. In return for this protection, the church was expected to be the mouthpiece of the state. The monarch was the head of the church and an Act of Settlement ensured that no Catholic – or no-one who has married a Catholic – could ever succeed to the throne. (This act, incidentally, is still in force, so if you've put down money on Prince William marrying Madonna, this might be a bad move.)

Legally, the crown appoints all bishops, most deans and has the patronage over a wide range of other appointments – including the appointments of many vicars to parishes. Although the governance of the C of E is supposed to be in the hands of General Synod, all measures have to be approved by Parliament before receiving assent from the Queen. And this is not a formality; in recent years Parliament has thrown out measures which have been sent to them – a fact which still rankles among many Anglicans.

I know what you will argue, Miles. You also say that, because it is established, the church's views are taken seriously. It has a platform from which to speak. They have all those bishops in the House of Lords. However, the future of the House of Lords is still a matter of considerable debate and it is worth noting that, as I write, at the latest meeting of the House of Lords reform committee, the bishops weren't represented.

Or perhaps you will argue that being 'established' means an entirely different thing down at 'ground level'. It gives you unique opportunities to reach out into people's lives. People view the church as part of the traditional heart of their towns or villages, they visit it at Christmas and Easter, they have their children baptised, they marry in the church; they are buried by the church.

These are, to my mind, more powerful arguments, but they are seriously undermined by the figures. Fewer and fewer people are being baptised into the church. Weddings are now barely half as popular as they were one hundred years ago. Catholic and Jewish weddings have remained stable, but Church of England weddings have fallen from a 68% rate in 1987 to a 22% rate today. The decline is such that the church has started to 'market' its 16,000 parish churches at National Wedding Shows. Whether this is because they are desperate to save souls or desperate to keep the revenue rolling in I am not sure.

Can't you see, Miles, that this whole establishment thing may be working against you? It's not as if your own members don't have misgivings. Many Anglicans view it as ludicrous that the Prime Minister and the House of Commons should have a say in who the Archbishop of Canterbury should be, while the thousands of people who attend Anglican Churches apparently have no say whatsoever.

And I think that, inside the church, establishment has had a pernicious effect. I have often had the subtle impression that the church has gone 'native'. This has been reflected in the apparatus and titles that have grown up around the church. I don't have to claim my own authority here. This is what your new Archbishop has said:

> The Anglican Church has bought very deeply into status. It's one of the most ambiguous elements in the whole of that culture – the concern with titles, the concern with the little differentiations, the different coloured buttons, as it were, the rosettes on the hat, as it used to be. And there have to be points where that gets challenged. There's something profoundly – I'll say it – anti-Christian in all of that. It's about guarding position, about fencing yourself in. And that is not quite what the Gospel is.
>
> ROWAN WILLIAMS, ARCHBISHOP OF CANTERBURY

When even the Archbishop of Canterbury starts to question whether the established church is a good thing, you know that the writing is on the wall.

Of course, the Anglican Church is not only politically and legally established; it is geographically established. The parish system was a way for the church to ensure that everyone in the land had spiritual oversight. But times have changed. While the parish system still has a validity in rural areas, where communities are much more clearly defined, in urban areas communities are not defined geographically.

Today's 'parishes' are more likely to be based on work, leisure or ethnic lines.

Yet parishes, too, are protected by law; it is illegal for anyone to plant a church in another parish without the consent of the incumbent. And vicars still have freehold, which means that they cannot be removed from post, except in very extreme cases.

All of which means that a failing parish can go on failing for years and years and years. The vicar cannot be removed, and other, more growth-oriented churches cannot establish new churches in the area. The fact is that the parish system, as it stands at the moment, is actually failing the church. It mitigates against church planting, and it rewards inadequate leadership with a job for life.

The Anglican Church has recognised a lot of these problems and is taking steps to change things. New churches are being developed which cut across parishes, or which operate on a more networked principle. There is a review underway of legal framework with a view to changing things. But that's the point, isn't it? Few things point up to the inability of the dear old C of E to respond to the present crisis in church attendance than the fact that, in order to push forward the idea of church planting, they are going to have to change the law.

Ever yours,
Stephen

PS: One further thought: the word parish has its origins in the Greek word *paroikia*, which actually means a group of resident aliens (*para* = 'near' and *oikos* = 'house', i.e. those who live next door). The original parishes then, were outsiders, groups of Christians who lived alongside their communities, but who were noticeably different to those around them. Once again, the issue seems to be a battle between a distinctive Christian presence or simply being a part of the fixtures and fittings.

tHe BoileD loBsteR

At first, what grabbed my attention
was the floor. The plastic floor of the egg-pod was semi-translu-
cent. Beneath my feet I could see wires and chips and motors, but
dimly, as if I was looking through icy water or frosted glass. And
beneath the workings of the vehicle, further through the misty
plastic, I could see a rapid blur of green, as if a painter had
smeared green oil paint across a canvas with a knife. I looked up.
Above waist height, where the egg-pod's shell was clear I could
see that we were travelling out of Oxford. But beneath my feet,
we appeared to be crossing over some kind of field.

I nudged Lydia and pointed down. 'Where's the road?
Where's the M40?'

'This is the M40,' said Lydia, fiddling with the buttons on her
silver air-suit. 'The pods are fired by a powerful magnet. Beneath
us, hidden below the surface is a huge magnetic strip which
pushes us away. Most roads had the strip laid down on top of
the surface, but on the motorways it was thought nicer to dis-
guise them. Bury them underground. And the net result was that,
without tyres to wear through, the motorways became overgrown with grass and moss.'

'You've literally let the grass grow under your feet.'

She smiled. 'Exactly. No-one noticed it at first, but gradually the M40 turned into a long, thin lawn.'

I did not return her smile.

'This is not the M40,' I snorted. 'For a start we haven't been overtaken by a travelling salesman going 110 miles per hour, while talking on his mobile phone. Nor are there any traffic jams.'

'No, our speed is automatically controlled. No-one can go faster than 120 kilometres per hour. And all the traffic is regulated so that jams no longer exist. Travel has got a lot better in the past few decades.'

'Not for the travelling salesman,' I said. 'You've taken all the fun out of his life.'

I looked at the carriageway on the other side of the road. There were pods of all shapes and sizes moving serenely along, just a few inches above the green ground. Some were small, with only room for one person, others were huge, and towed behind them large boxes full of goods. Some were brightly coloured, garish blobs of lemon yellow and fluorescent green; others – particularly the bigger white eggs, were dirtied by their journeys or covered with advertising logos and carrying a 'Well Hovered?' sticker on the back. All moved in unison, a strange ballet, silent and serene.

For some reason, the sight made me angry and upset. Perhaps I was jealous of this world, with its calm, congestion-less motorway travel. 'It's not the M40 . . . ,' I muttered again. 'It shouldn't be this way.'

Lydia smiled. 'You've had a shock,' she said. 'It must be difficult for you, coming to terms with all these changes.'

'It's not the novelty I can't cope with,' I replied. 'It's the guilt.'

'Guilt?'

'I feel ... responsible. I spent a lot of my time criticising the church; mocking it, challenging it. But I never thought one day it wouldn't be there. I never thought it would disappear. It's like losing an old friend. An annoying, old-fashioned, stubborn, idiotic friend, admittedly, but nevertheless ...'

'That's the point of this journey, I think,' said Lydia. 'Maybe when you get back you know that you have to do more than make fun. Maybe the point of this journey is that you can get your friendship back.'

The rest of the journey passed in peace. Despite the speed we were going, the pod hardly wobbled at all. What movement there was was very gentle. I sat there, soothed by the movement and the comfort of the deep, padded seats. Pretty soon, I dozed off, and when I woke, we were off the motorway and passing through streets and houses, at the edges of the vast urban sprawl that was London. As far as I could see, the houses looked much as they always had, except for a wide proliferation of silver, mirrored solar panels on doors and roofs, covering the houses in shimmering scales like a fish.

Lydia reached forward and punched a button on the console in front of her. We passed by a row of rather dilapidated shops, turned a gentle corner and then drew quietly to a halt in front of a pair of broken and rusty iron gates. With a hiss, the pod dropped to the ground, where it sat on three small, stubby feet. The hatch opened and we climbed out.

Outside the air-conditioned pod, the atmosphere was close and humid. Beyond the gates lay a broken and disused drive, crowded and jostled by wild and overgrown vegetation. The heat, the greenness, the dilapidation gave the place an eerie, almost tropical feel. I felt like an extra in *Apocalypse Now*. Whenever 'now' was.

'Where are we?'

'Don't you recognise it?'

I looked at the gates. My mind seemed as overgrown as the landscape I was looking at. Then, slowly, from deep within the vegetation, a memory slithered out.

'Wasn't this a Bible college? I remember ... friends came here to study. To become ...' The words trailed away as I realised why it was forlorn and abandoned. No need for ministers now. No posts to fill. No congregations to preach to.

There was a sign on the gates.

**Building Acquired
By MicroSpore Genetic Industries.
Building Better People Through Design.
Keep Out!!!!**

Lydia took one look at the sign.

'They're very fond of exclamation marks, aren't they?' she asked. Suddenly, she reached out and ripped it down. Then she took a few steps back, then, with surprising strength, strode forward and gave the rusty gates a kick that would have felled a sixteen-stone prop forward. The gates didn't so much open, as surrender.

She turned to me and smiled. 'Shall we go in?' she enquired, sweetly.

'Whatever you say,' I said.

Inside the grounds, the undergrowth was dense and difficult. Whoever owned the site now, it was clear that they needed to employ a gardener. Or possibly an explorer.

'So what happened?' I asked, pushing through some enormous, clinging vine. 'Doesn't anybody study theology nowadays?'

'Oh yes,' she replied. 'Only it tends to be part of the university's anthropology department.'

'Anthropology?'

She took a vicious karate chop at a six-foot-high weed, which collapsed immediately. 'Yes. You know, rites and rituals and beliefs that sort of thing. Or you can do some of it as part of an archaeology degree. Ancient languages and customs.'

'Archaeology?'

She looked at me, rather surprised. 'I should have thought you would have been pleased. You were always rather critical of theologians, as I recall. You used to say that if you asked five theologians the same question you would get six answers and a new denomination.'

'Yes, but ... well, it's not that theologians weren't discussing important things. When you look at it, theology is grappling with some really important questions; they're just rubbish at talking about them in a way that people understand. I think all theologians should be forced to write a summary of their research which could be understood by ordinary people ...' I trailed off. Lydia wasn't listening to me but was staring at the ground.

Suddenly she paused and looked carefully about her. 'Be careful,' said Lydia, 'There are snakes around here.'

I looked down uncertainly at the dense grass that hid my feet. 'Snakes? In London?'

'Happened a few years ago. A bunch of animal rights protesters broke into the zoo and liberated a batch of coral snakes; venomous snakes from America. It was all a bit of a mistake really. The police think the activists smashed the wrong case and that they were really trying to free some rare Argentinian spotted newts. They found them the next morning, lying dead with a very surprised look on their face.'

'How can you tell if an Argentinian spotted newt is surprised?' I asked. 'I mean, I shouldn't think they have the most expressive faces ...'

'Not the newts, the protesters!' she said. 'The newts were fine. The protesters were all dead. They'd let out the wrong reptile.'

'Oh.'

'Of course in your day they would simply have frozen to death in the winter.'

There was a pause. 'I know our winters were cold,' I said, 'but even so, not many protesters ever froze to death ...'

'Not the protesters, the coral snakes!' She looked at me with an expression that must have been very similar to that of the coral snakes before they tucked into their rescuers. 'The coral snakes escaped,' she said, slowly. 'And they've thrived, because, you know, since global warming, the winters are much more mild.'

'Oh.' I thought again. 'So what happened to the newts?'

'I give up,' she muttered. She took a vicious sideswipe at a large, overgrown bush and marched off through the undergrowth.

I followed her as best I could. It was hard work and the sweat on my face stung in my eyes.

'It's so hot,' I muttered.

'I told you,' said Lydia, delivering a particularly nasty kidney punch to an unsuspecting shrub, 'global warming.'

'Ah yes. Global warming,' I said. 'I've been meaning to ask about that. What effect did it have? Was the place sunnier?'

'Britain? No, of course not. But the rain was a lot warmer. And you got some exotic new weeds. And some new species. Crocodiles in the lakes, that sort of thing. Anyway, we didn't come here to talk about climate change – although perhaps we did in a way.' She paused and for the first time seemed to be breathing heavily.

'When the climate changes you either adapt or die,' she said. 'But first you have to recognise that the temperature is changing.'

'What do you mean?'

'It's like the roads. You don't realise that the grass is growing until one day you wake up and the motorway is overgrown. You don't realise the gates are rusty until one day you can't force them open anymore. The lobsters don't realise that the water is heating up until they are too tired to move ...'

There was a pause. 'You lost me on the last bit,' I said.

She looked at me, surprised. 'Haven't you ever boiled a lobster?' she asked.

I laughed. 'No. Funnily enough that was not one of the regular meals in the Page household. We were more what you might call a 'fish finger' household. Occasionally, for a treat, we would open a can of sardines. But only, you understand, on a special occasion.'

She stared at me. 'Of course,' she muttered. 'I keep forgetting. It's just that now, lobsters are pretty common fare. When the sea stocks of fish dwindled we had to pour more money into intensive fish farming. So we have loads of stuff like lobsters, but you can't get a herring for love nor money.'

'You're what might be called hard of herring.'

This time her stare was longer. 'We have a difficult enough task ahead of us, without puns like that,' she said. 'Anyway, to return to lobsters, the most humane way of killing them is to put them in cold water and gradually bring it to the boil. The lobsters just go to sleep.'

There was a long pause while I tried to see where this conversation was going. It seemed as meandering and impenetrable as our attempts to get through the vegetation.

'Oh,' I said, at last. 'Very interesting. Does the same thing happen to newts?'

'LOOK, FORGET THE NEWTS!' she shouted. 'JUST PAY ATTENTION TO THE LOBSTERS, RIGHT? IT'S LOBSTERS WE'RE TALKING ABOUT NOW. LOBSTERS! UNDERSTAND?'

For a moment I felt a surge of sympathy for the gates.

'Right,' I said. 'Lobsters. In water. Being boiled.'

'Yes,' she said, calming down. 'Lobsters. And when you put them in cold water and bring it to the boil, they stay there. They die. They don't realise anything is wrong. They simply cannot tell that the climate is changing.'

She suddenly pushed aside a big bush and there, rising out of the weeds and the brambles was the broken, battered old building that had once housed the Bible college.

'Behold,' said Lydia, with a gesture. 'The biggest lobster in the world.'

→•←

It had been, in its time, a splendid building. Modernist in style, with clean, red brick, it had somehow embodied the optimism that filled the church in the post-war years. But now its once magnificent entrance was crumbling; now its big oak doors were boarded up. The ivy clad walls were more 'ivy' than 'wall' and the windows were black shadows, encrusted with shards of broken glass.

We walked up to the steps, now cracked and uneven, the concrete stained and blackened with neglect. This building had once been full of students, now it stood, empty and eerie. Fluttering in its empty rooms I could hear the past, beating its ghostly wings.

'I remember this place,' I said, sadly. 'It was good. It changed people. It was forward thinking. Friends of mine studied here. It taught good things ...'

I looked up at the skeleton of the building. It was a corpse now, a cadaver, waiting for dissection or burial.

'The problem with the colleges wasn't what they taught the students, it was what they didn't teach,' replied Lydia. 'There were lots of people studying here every year, but the real question is, were they studying the right things?'

We sat down on two large blocks of concrete and stared at the building. Lydia turned to me.

'What do you think the single most important skill is in leading a church?'

'I've never really thought about it.'

'Oh yes you have. You sat and thought about it in every church you were a part of. Every church you went into, every leader you met you were looking to them for one thing.'

'Which was what?'

She looked at me. 'Leadership,' she said. 'That's what you need to lead a church. That's what you need to take the people forward. You need to be a leader. You need leadership skills. And what did we teach them? Theology.' She started to laugh. 'I remember talking to a curate who came to our church back when you were still alive,' she said. 'Back at the turn of the century. He told me how much training they had on management skills. Guess.'

I shrugged. 'Well, by then even the colleges should have got their act together ... so I'd guess about ten sessions or something?'

'One morning.'

'One?'

'One morning out of three years. That's all. One morning in management skills, to train people who were going to have to come out and chair meetings, build teams, organise volunteers, set goals, manage their time, train others. One morning!' She wiped her eyes. 'They spent a heck of a lot of time learning about ancient Israel. It's just a shame they couldn't squeeze in a little more about modern Britain.'

'Yes, but these were Bible colleges. You are surely not suggesting that we shouldn't teach theology to those who are going to preach the Bible.'

'Of course not. But let's look at the assumptions behind the question. The assumption is that those who teach are always going to be the ones who lead. We so combined the teaching and preaching role with the leadership role, that we couldn't imagine one without the other. Those who lead the churches had to be the ones who preach. But why should it be that just because you can put together a neat three-pointer on "The Purpose of the Table Lamp in the Old Testament", then you automatically have the abilities to lead a group of fifty volunteers?'

She sighed. 'Of course leaders need to be theologically and biblically literate. But more than that, you have to be able to manage a team. The ministerial training of your time was geared to those who felt they had a gift for teaching. But as soon as they got out of college and into the real world, they discovered that teaching was only a small part of the picture. They were leaders and they were suddenly handed roles and responsibilities for which they were ill-equipped and with which they simply could not cope.' She paused. 'In a way they didn't read the Bible well enough. You see, one of the things you get from reading the Old Testament is that the prophets and the priests were not necessarily the kings.'

'So where should they have looked? What kinds of skills should we have been giving them?'

'They should have looked around them. Outside of the church there were many organisations with visionary leaders and entrepreneurs. Many of the people leading these were Christians. But did the colleges call on them to pass on that expertise to their students? Did the ministerial training colleges call experts from the world of industry or communication or teaching in to teach their students? Rarely if ever. No, they might have been leading successful organisations, but they didn't have a theology degree. So, of course, what they had to say wasn't important.'

'Well, I know people who would argue that the church was a successful organisation. I mean it survived for two thousand years.'

She stared at me. Suddenly into the undergrowth I thought I saw a flash of purple and red, a reptilian slither that disappeared as soon as it had arrived.

'You know,' said Lydia. 'The dinosaurs were the most successful species ever. Right up until the point where they suddenly became extinct.'

There was silence. It was very still in the clearing around the old building. No wind. Just birdsong and the buzzing of insects. The background noise of life; of many different species, competing for space and food.

'All right,' I said, 'so many of the colleges weren't teaching the right things. But what about the students themselves?'

'What do you mean?'

'Well, it's not just the subjects, is it? It's also a question of the raw material. When the great preacher Charles Spurgeon set up his college in the nineteenth century he started in a back room in his church. And those who were allowed to study had to demonstrate two things – first that they were preaching in their church, second that they had made converts. Nothing more. He wanted to know whether they had the practical skills necessary to make the most of what they had to learn. I don't know how often colleges tested the practical abilities of candidates or whether they were only interested in how many exams they'd passed. The result was often that people came out trained as ministers but without some of the basic skills that you need to do the job. You'd be amazed at the number of people who end up running churches who have practically no people-skills whatsoever.'

'Yes, well, there's something in that,' admitted Lydia. 'Certainly I wonder whether the colleges really made sure that their candidates had the right qualifications for church leadership. I don't mean academic qualifications – they were covered well enough. You could easily see the certificates and read the grades. And, of course, they always tested for orthodoxy. But other qualifications and attributes? They are harder to judge because most of them can only be seen in the field.'

She thought for a moment. 'Which was a problem, really. I mean hands-on skills can be developed, but only if there is something to get your hands on. Only in a real-life placement. And I'm not sure how many students were given meaningful on-the-ground experience. Placements, you see, are never enough – what can a six-week placement really teach you about handling responsibility and leading a church? Long-term placements are the only thing that really give students a grounding in the realities of their work. On-the-job training; in post.'

'What could they have done?'

'Well, simply looking around would have been something. They could have taken a walk out of the college gates or through the college door. Look into the real world, see what skills were needed, how they could best communicate their message.'

'Environment scanning,' I said. 'I remember learning it on a management course. It's just a posh management-speak for looking around you.'

'Exactly. But you see all those are functions of leadership. First, the raw talent, second the hands-on experience and third, the ability to look at what your enemy is doing – and steal his good ideas.'

She smiled.

'There were lots of tools that the clergy could have found so useful,' she said. 'Vision statements. Do you remember those? A feature of all good organisations in your time. Vision statements. Aims and objectives. Basic management tools. But how many churches didn't have them? And how many rejected them because they were "too worldly"? And so they blundered on. They had sermon after sermon, knowledge till it was pouring out of their ears. But no idea of where they were going, what they were supposed to be doing or how they would know if they actually got there. And these places carried on teaching their doctrine, their theology, their church history, while all around the world was boiling.'

There was a silence. Something rustled in the long grass.

'Look,' I said, 'when we started out this journey you told me that the real reason why the church died out in this country was because Christians weren't different enough, because we were too much like the rest of the world around us. Now you're telling me that we weren't like the world enough. You can't have it both ways.'

She shook her head. 'You take the good things and reject the bad,' she snapped. 'You learn the skills. Look at the tools the world uses to get its message across. Look at how they organise themselves. And then do it better.'

A pigeon rose. Cumbersome, flapping from the undergrowth.

'As harmless as doves,' said Lydia. 'And as wise as serpents.'

Suddenly there was a pain. A sudden rustling beneath my feet. A red line, like blood, slipping away down the steps.

'Talking of serpents,' I said. 'I think I've just been bitten on the leg.'

And with that I passed into blackness.

Dear Miles,

This manuscript is taking me along some pretty unexpected highways and byways, I must admit. I hardly thought that I would be spending my time scanning the Internet, studying the online syllabuses (syllabi? syllabubs?) of ministerial training colleges. (I think Page rather underestimates the importance of academic training, but then, I would say that, wouldn't I?)

I am not sure that I am knowledgeable enough to analyse the truth of Page's argument that colleges need to teach more management and business skills. All I have learnt I have learnt from watching those television programmes where a high-ranking businessman visits a business in trouble, tells them what's wrong, and then watches while the firm rejects every particle of his advice. But I have done some checking up. Whatever the rather fevered fantasy world he has created (snakes? in London?) the statistics do rather bear out the lack of emphasis of these kind of skills.

A look at the course content for seventeen of the best-known Bible colleges reveals that nine have courses on leadership. Of these only two mention the dread word 'management', and two offer teaching on 'Leadership and

Teamwork'. The fact that over 50% of the sample are teaching the subject might seem to undermine Page's argument. But in *every one* of these colleges, 'leadership' is an optional module. Not a single student has to take it. Thus, it would be entirely possible to study at any of these colleges and never touch directly on the topic of leadership.

It is possible, of course, that these modules are some of the most heavily attended of all the options; but I fear that too many prospective ministers and ordinands opt out. They spend two or three years training to lead a church without being given any training in how to lead. The message being given out is simple; leadership is optional.

Perhaps courses should take more account of what parishioners and congregations want and need. Are congregations ever asked to comment on the training of their pastors, vicars or ministers? Do ministerial training colleges ever make detailed, sustained efforts to follow up their students as they enter new posts, to see what skills are missing and to integrate that data back into their training?

In the Anglican system there is, at least, the curacy, which allows not only for on-the-job training but should in theory allow both congregation and clergy to feedback on their student's process. Yet this does not often happen. The vicar might feedback, but I'm not convinced that the views of the congregation are ever sought, at least not in a structured way.

This would not be such a huge issue were it not for the fact that congregations do have very different ideas about what training their clergy need. The best illustration of this is a survey which was done in America. Students, professors and church-goers were asked what ministerial candidates should learn. The professors put knowledge top of the agenda. The students thought that learning practical skills was the most important.

And the churches thought that the most important area of learning was relationships; that the ability to nurture, to create and to encourage relationships was the most important part of ministerial training.

Of course you need all three. But it demonstrates that if you do not listen to your customers, you are in danger of ending up with a product that is at best only two-thirds as good as it should be.

So Page's argument may have some weight. Personally, however, I have always been more concerned about the way in which we train students, as much as the course content. I have seen some surveys which estimated that it is impossible in college to provide people with more than around 50% of what they need to do the job properly. In which case, it becomes vitally important to secure ongoing in-post training following their entrance into the big wide world of ministry.

Good, relevant 'on-the-job' training is what's really needed in my opinion. And congregations have a role to play here. What churches need, perhaps, are people who will ask the right kind of questions: What areas are we weak in? What training is there to help us address those areas of weakness? Will that training help us to do our jobs better?

Of course, this training is available for lay people as well. And one of the big gaps in Page's account is that he concentrates too much on ordained, full-time clergy. But declining church attendance means declining numbers of paid clergy. In nearly all denominations the number of trainees is declining. In some dioceses around 30% of the clergy are Ordained Local Ministers.

There is nothing new in this. The early church leaders were all lay leaders to some extent. Paul kept making tents; Peter probably kept his hand in with the fishing net. But I'm not sure that the church has fully woken up to the implications.

First it means that ordained ministers and vicars must become trainers of others. Part of their training, therefore, will have to be how to train others. This will not be optional; it will be a requirement of their trade that they pass on their skills to as many other people as possible. Skills will only be given to them on the understanding that they pass those skills on.

Secondly, lay leadership training will have to change. Some denominations eschew any formal training in this area – particularly in areas such as the new churches, where authority is given to lay people who can demonstrate the abilities in preaching, administration, leadership, etc. Other denominations – officially at least – have a complex system of grades and training schemes. The Anglican Church, rather typically, has a plethora of different grades and titles, including Non-Stipendiary Ministers, Ordained Local Ministers (formerly Non-Stipendiary Local Ministers), Readers, Authorised Pastoral Assistants . . . and so on. Many Anglican Churches ignore these completely, giving responsibility happily to anyone who can prove they can do it. Others insist that their lay ministers pass the official training. (And don't all those titles still smack of 'imperial' control. It's not just about training, it's about authorisation and accreditation; it's about the centre retaining control.

I wonder how many good potential leaders will be prepared to jump through all these hoops just so that they can become officially recognised?)

Lay leadership will surely have to become less centralised, more local and more 'on the job'. Churches will make their own selections, appointments and training at local level. The idea of lay people needing central authorisation to act in certain ways in churches will die, because local people will be more in charge of their church. I ought to point out, in case you think that I am solely bashing the Anglicans, this is not confined to them. For centuries the Baptist churches selected their ministers locally. Usually the church recognised the calling and then invited the local churches to confirm that calling. It was only relatively recently that the denomination began to insist on central approval and accreditation.

The truth is that empowering the laity automatically means disempowering the authorities. Give the laity more responsibility and they will take more authority. You can't shift one without the other.

We're already seeing this. I know of many Anglican Churches where the whole congregation is more involved. In many churches the congregation say together parts of the service originally restricted to the clergy: the opening collect, the confession and the prayer of humble access, etc. Hundreds if not thousands of churches use preachers who are not licensed lay readers, and assistants at communion who have not gone through any official process. They're just part of the community. Partly this is due to the fact that most vicars are overworked, partly it's due to a simple recognition that it's good to have everyone more involved in the service.

There is one final implication of lay involvement that few Anglican Churches are facing up to. Since you started me on this little project, I have read many books on church attendance and on different models for the future. Most of them argue strongly for the expansion of the role of the laity among the Church of England, but they all seem to fall short of the logical conclusion. They argue that lay ministry is the future, except in one crucial area. In the Anglican Church, as I understand it, the situation is that the prayer of consecration (or thanksgiving) is the one part of the Lord's Supper which only the priest may say.

The corollary of this is that in some areas, where priests are often in charge of a number of parishes, the poor incumbent has to bomb around the countryside leading four, five, six or more communion services every Sunday. Since the Anglican tradition is that there should be weekly Holy Communion in all parish churches, it puts a ridiculous burden on an already over-stretched employee. Incidentally, this limitation is not put on any of the other sacraments, all of which can be carried out by anyone in an emergency. As I understand it, in an emergency a nurse could administer baptism to a dying person, but you can't have Communion in a parish if the priest is ill. It also gives out an unfortunate message; that 'priests are the really special people and you can't have a real church without one.'

I think in the end, people will grasp the nettle – or the chalice to be more precise. Already there are many Anglicans who serve Communion to each other, perhaps as part of youth outreach, perhaps as part of house groups. They don't see any need for the official figure to be there, and many vicars prefer to turn a blind eye rather than create a scene.

I know what you will say, Miles. You will say that practicalities shouldn't drive doctrine. I say that in the future there will be loads of churches without priests. Are they to be churches without Communion as well?

Lay involvement is a dangerous animal, Miles. Like the rather fanciful coral snakes in Page's story; smash the case and let it loose and it might just turn around and bite you. But the laity do not thrive in captivity; keep them caged and the church will wither and die.

I will write again soon.

All the best,
Stephen

PS: You might be interested to know that the snake Page refers to is probably the eastern coral snake, or *micrurs fulvius fulvius*, to give it its Latin name. Or you might not. I just wanted to prove that I'm still doing my research!

pHysiciaN heAl youRself

When I woke there was a bright light shining in my face.

'Where am I?' I asked. 'What happened?' I tried to move, but something was enclosing me, wrapping around me like a cocoon. I couldn't move my arms or my legs. With difficulty I managed to raise my head for a moment to see what was holding me. I was lying on some kind of stretcher, wrapped tight in what looked like a large amount of heavily padded silver foil. Suddenly I understood exactly what an oven-ready chicken felt like.

'What's happening to me . . .' My mouth felt dry and my throat was sore.

'Please don't talk,' said a gentle, musical, yet strangely annoying voice. 'I will keep you in stasis, until we reach the hospital.'

'Who are you?'

'Your medi-suit.'

'My suit? My suit is talking to me?'

'Your medi-suit.' Out of the corner of my eye I could see a small silver grille in the front of the suit, out of which this oily voice was oozing. 'I have been given the privilege of caring for you during this journey. I am monitoring your condition. You are satisfactory.' There was a pause. 'Although if you ask me, you could stand to lose a few pounds.' It was like listening to a cross between a nanny and the worst TV presenter imaginable. 'How are your bowel movements?' asked the suit.

'My what?'

'Your movements,' replied the suit. 'Are you regular?'

'I always knew going to Bible college was bad for your health,' I muttered. 'But I never knew it was going to be like this.'

Lydia's face loomed into view. She looked down at me. 'Don't panic,' she said. 'It's only a bite. We're used to them by now. We'll soon be at the Self-Heal Unit. The medi-suit will keep you okay.'

'I certainly will,' trilled the suit. 'And while I am caring for you, I would like to sing excerpts from the twentieth-century musical-film *Mary Poppins.*'

'I don't believe this . . .'

'Oh, a spoonful of sugar,' sang the medi-suit, 'helps the sedative go down . . .'

'Shut up!' I started to thrash about inside the suit. 'I'm not in the mood for this. I've been catapulted through time, bitten by a snake and now I'm being serenaded by an overgrown duvet . . .'

'You are becoming agitated,' said the medi-suit, breaking off from its warbling. 'I will give you a sedative.'

'I don't want a sedative . . .'

'Now, now, medi-suit knows best.'

It was no use. I could feel myself growing drowsy again. As I drifted off, dim fragments of memory rearranged themselves in my brain. I could see the black iron gates of the theological college and I was trying to open them, but just as I shook them, the iron bars turned into one, huge, black, oily, undulating snake, which suddenly started to coil around my legs. Up and up it sped, in a moment engulfing my arms, legs, body, neck. And as it reached my face, it raised its head, fangs dripping venom, reptilian eyes gleaming, only it wasn't the head of a snake, it was the face of Lydia and she hissed 'You're never going to get this, are you?' and then it wasn't Lydia anymore but a huge snakeskin handbag which began singing the greatest hits of Julie Andrews and then, mercifully, everything went black.

When I next woke I was lying on a kind of padded bench in a large, bright white room. The walls were so bright they hurt my eyes. I was awake and my arm was moving, only I wasn't moving it. I looked down and saw that Lydia was inserting my hand into a kind of metal sleeve which was attached to the bed.

'What's going on?' I croaked.

'Please relax,' said my suit, in a voice which instantly made me about as unrelaxed as it's possible to be, 'you are being plugged in.'

'What do you mean?' I panicked. 'I don't want to be plugged in to anything thank you. Let me go. What are you doing to me?'

'Now don't be such a cry-baby,' scolded the suit. 'It's for your own good. It won't hurt a bit.'

'When this is over I'm going to personally put you through the boil wash,' I muttered. 'And then I'm going to run you through a mangle for extra measure.'

Once my hand was in the socket, I felt something metal contract around it and hold me.

'Reading your DNA details now . . . ,' said the medi-suit. There was a long pause. 'Well that doesn't compute at all,' said the suit eventually. It sniffed in annoyance.

'What's the matter?' I asked.

'According to your DNA topography you are Nick Page.'

'Yes.'

'And you are also dead.'

'Ah.'

The suit sounded personally aggrieved.

'According to central records you died twenty-two, oh-seven, 2031. Cause of death . . .' There was another long pause. 'Good grief,' said the medi-suit. It sounded shocked. 'That must have been upsetting.'

'What? What was upsetting?'

'Never mind all that now,' interrupted Lydia.

'But I want to know what was upsetting! I want to know the details!'

'No. I don't think you do.'

'This is most inconvenient,' said the suit. 'Oh, why do you humans make things so complicated? How can I possibly treat you if you're dead?'

'I should have thought about this earlier,' muttered Lydia.

'What's the problem?'

'Everything you do now is linked into the central database,' she explained. 'If you're dead, you don't have access to it. So, no money, no travel and no healthcare. But I think we can fix it.'

She reached into her jacket and pulled out a small, rectangular card, like a credit card, but made out of some kind of flexible metal. Then she swiped it through a small gap in the medi-suit's read-out panel. The suit beeped twice.

'Override detected,' it said. 'DNA updating. Registry confirmed.'

'What's going on?'

'I'm just changing your identity,' said Lydia. 'So that the suit thinks you're still alive. That way you'll get treatment.'

'Changing my identity? But I don't want . . .'

'Look,' she snapped, 'if the suit thinks you're dead it won't treat you, will it? It won't bother healing a dead person. So, if you want to live, I suggest you shut up.' She paused and patted my head. 'Anyway,' she continued, 'it's only temporary. Only for a moment.'

There was a bleep from the medi-suit. 'Identity confirmed. How are you feeling Brigadier Protheroe?'

There was a pause.

'Brigadier Protheroe?' I asked. Lydia looked slightly embarrassed.

'It was a rush job,' she said. 'I had to take what I could get.' She leaned over to the medi-suit. 'Euro-creds,' she said.

'Euro-creds approved,' bleeped the suit. 'Payment to be debited from the account of Brigadier Samantha Protheroe.'

There was a *long* pause.

'Samantha,' I clarified.

'Yes,' Lydia replied, looking even more uncomfortable. 'Still, look on the bright side. You had a long and distinguished military career.'

'You've turned me into a woman!' I hissed. 'Surely someone's going to notice.'

She shook her head. 'Oh no, I shouldn't think so. Things have got very confused gender-wise since your time,' she thought for a moment. 'Actually they were pretty confused in your time, weren't they? But things have got even more difficult.'

'Payment confirmed,' said the medi-suit. 'Treatment will proceed.' And I suddenly felt my hand grow hot within the metal glove, as though I had dipped it into a bath.

I looked at Lydia. 'You have to pay?'

'Of course. You don't think the Health Service survived, do you?'

'Well, I sort of hoped ...'

'Oh no,' she said. 'Everyone's a consumer and everything's a product these days. If you don't have the money, you don't get the cure.'

I looked around me. All around the walls there were trolleys like the one I was lying on, but no-one else was using them.

'Where are we?'

'SHU. Self-Heal Unit. It's kind of like Accident and Emergency, only without the blood and hysteria.'

'And the overcrowding apparently. Where is everyone?'

She laughed. 'Oh it's all computerised now,' she said. 'We don't use people any more. All the diagnosis and treatment is electronically administered. You can see a doctor if you like, but it's always more expensive.' She paused. 'The funny thing is that loads of people still choose that, even though all the doctor does, on the whole, is lie you on a trolley and plug you in.'

'I guess it's the personal touch.'

'Yes. Of course, the whole idea behind these self-treats was to avoid getting people involved, largely because there were fewer people around. Mainly these units were created because of the difficulty of getting people to work in the public services. One of the less-foreseen effects of the collapse of Christian values.'

I grimaced. 'I don't see the link.'

'People used to talk about vocation when they talked about those jobs. They used to see them as a calling.'

I snorted. 'Yes, well, the only difference between a job and a vocation is that you can pay people less in a vocation.'

'No. A vocation came out of a moral vision. Look,' she continued, 'Christianity always taught people the importance of service and sacrifice. It encouraged people to serve their fellow humans. But when Christianity faded, that view faded as well. The prevailing moral climate of your time was one of self-interest.

And in that kind of society it becomes more and more difficult to fill jobs that require self-sacrifice.'

'You're not claiming that the crisis in the Health Service was directly attributable to the decline of Christianity?'

'Not wholly – but it was all part of the mix. Even though Christianity had been declining for decades, there was still an acceptance of some of its values – the idea of service being one of them. When those go, then all you get is a religion of self. So instead, the government was reduced to trying to teach people citizenship. We had to teach them how to be citizens of earth because they no longer believed they were citizens of heaven.'

'You seem to be arguing that people will put up with lousy pay and poor working conditions as long as they believe strongly enough in self-sacrifice.'

She sniffed. 'I know you're ill, but do try to listen. I'm not justifying the poor pay or conditions or anything like that. I'm saying that a lot of people went into these kind of jobs because the moral framework in which they were raised encouraged them to serve their fellow human beings. Even when specific Christian beliefs began to fade and die, there was still an appreciation of the value of self-sacrifice and mercy. But eventually – when the only moral framework was "look after number one" – then the idea of "vocations" disappears. So it becomes merely a question of pay and conditions. That's one of the reasons that in your time it became so hard to recruit teachers and nurses and doctors.' She looked thoughtful for a moment. 'You never see these things in advance, do you?' she said. 'But losing a Christian presence in Britain meant so much more than losing a few buildings or some blokes dressed in funny costume. It meant losing a whole moral framework; a whole way of looking at the world.'

I tried to think. Lydia was right. But how many Christians of my day, I wondered, had already abandoned that moral framework themselves? How many of them had spent just as much time chasing the pay rise and raising themselves on the backs of other people? I closed my eyes. My head was groggy and there was a pain in my leg.

'Are you sure this is working?' I asked. 'I can't feel any change . . .'

'Don't worry,' said Lydia. 'These units might be irritating, but they are very efficient.'

I smiled. 'I always found the two qualities to be very similar.'

'That's just because you were totally disorganised,' said Lydia. 'As I recall you were an administrative black hole. We always get irritated by people whose qualities show up our own faults.'

'I don't think that's fair,' I said. 'Anyway, what do you know about my administrative abilities?'

'Not much,' she admitted. 'But let's face it, it was one of the reasons for your death. If you hadn't been in such a hurry, you might have noticed the water-buffalo . . .' She let the sentence trail off as she realised that she had drifted into forbidden subject matter. 'Still, let's not worry about that now,' she said, trying to be soothing.

'Hurry?' I asked. 'Water-buffalo?'

'I shouldn't have mentioned it,' said Lydia curtly. 'Anyway, it looks like your treatment has been successful.'

She pointed to a small panel on the wall near me, where green lights were flashing in unison. Strangely a small display panel was flashing the word 'Goal!' and some small speakers started to blare out Queen's 'We Are the Champions'. I looked at Lydia. She shrugged. 'They're trying to make the whole process more user-friendly and informal,' she replied.

Suddenly my suit started speaking to me again.

'I have identified your illness, Brigadier Protheroe,' it said, 'and it has been dealt with successfully.'

'Thank you.'

'You're welcome. However I ought to point out a number of other body anomalies that I have detected. For a start, your testosterone level is dangerously high for a seventy-year-old woman.'

There was a pause. A much longer pause than before.

'I thought you said it wouldn't notice my gender?' I hissed.

'Well, it's not much to worry about,' said Lydia.

'More importantly,' continued the medi-suit. 'I can't help noticing that your left leg has grown back. Which is unusual to say the least.'

There was a huge, enormous, gigantic pause.

Lydia looked at me. 'Just a minor detail,' she said, eventually.

'A minor detail! It might be a minor detail to you, but I'm now a seventy-year-old, one-legged ex-army brigadier called Samantha! That hardly counts as "minor" in my book.'

'Oh for heaven's sake, stop moaning,' snapped Lydia. 'I suppose you'd have preferred it if I'd left you back in the college.'

'That is not the point and you know it,' I replied.

'You're an ungrateful fool.'

'And you're a supercilious, pompous old woman.'

'Don't you talk to me that way, young man.'

'I am not a "young man",' I shouted. 'I am an old woman. And I'm probably your commanding officer!'

There was a silence while we glared at one another.

'Would you like me to point out several more areas where your health could be improved?' asked the suit.

'No!' I shouted. 'Just leave me alone! Just all of you leave me alone!'

I pulled my hand out of the metal sleeve, sat up, grabbed the tab at the front of the suit and ripped it off. The suit immediately began to deflate with a sad kind of hiss and, as I threw it onto the floor, a small, plaintive voice said; 'She's right, you are ungrateful ...'

Lydia didn't say anything. She just knelt down and began to fold up the suit. Then she carefully replaced it in its protective bag.

'There's no need to take it out on the equipment,' she said. 'People need to use these things after you.'

I shook my head.

'I'm sorry,' I said. 'I'm sorry. Things just got a bit ... well, you know.'

She looked up at me, and for the first time I noticed that she had tears in her eyes. She had been so unemotional up till now, so restrained, so terribly English.

'This isn't easy for me, either,' she said. 'You don't have the monopoly on guilt. We're all in this together.'

'Yes,' I said. 'I know.' I gestured towards the suit. 'I suppose it was that thing. It was like being suffocated by a psychotic nanny. I can see why people prefer the doctors.'

'Yes,' agreed Lydia. She stood up, and the old Lydia returned; steely, unemotional, matter-of-fact. And obviously keen to change the subject. 'That's why not many people come here. They all prefer to pay more and see a doctor or a nurse or the Local General Herbalist.'

I shook my head. 'I'm sorry?'

'Oh you can get all kinds of alternative therapies in the National Health now. Herbalism, acupuncture, gem-therapy. . . .

Providing, of course, you can pay for it. Anyway, the point is that people prefer to pay more and go to those clinics, than come here and be treated by a machine. People need people. They want to talk about their illness, not just obey the commands of some electronic machine.'

'I heard that . . . ,' said a muffled voice from within the plastic packaging. 'I think, speaking as highly technologically advanced clothing I know what is best for the patient.' Lydia swiftly poked the bag, and the suit's complaining voice dwindled away.

'Sorry,' she said. 'Forgot to turn it off. Anyway,' she continued, 'you can't replace real care and attention. People in your time were crying out for it. Crying out for someone to care for them. They were desperate for relationships, for someone to say they cared. And what did they get? Chatlines. Therapists. Professional friends. Oh, our society was too busy to be friends; we preferred to employ others to do it for us.'

'A bit of a sweeping statement. Therapy wasn't quite as simple as that.'

'No. Perhaps not. But the point is that nothing beats a listening ear and a shoulder to cry on. Nothing communicates God's love better than one of his people putting it into action. People wanted someone to listen to them, someone to pay attention to their fears and their anxieties; to tell them that it was all going to be all right, to tell them that they mattered. They needed someone to show them that God loves them. And who better than the church to do that? You can try to replace friendship and care with artificial constructs, but nothing replaces the real thing.'

'Well, as I recall the church did do a lot of practical care. Missionaries, aid and development, social care organisations and all that . . .'

'Yes, of course. But it was also really needed at the local level – in the towns and the villages. That's where the church could make a huge difference. But so often what we wanted to do was to talk rather than act. We were too busy telling people what was wrong with them, telling them what to think, to listen to what they really needed. We had so much doctrine and dogma to stuff them with, we never noticed they were scared and desperate and lonely.'

She shrugged.

'I mean, it's not rocket science, is it? The key message of Christianity is so simple. God loves you. Everything else springs out of that simple fact – all the other stuff about forgiveness and redemption and prayer and eternal life. It all springs from three little words: "God loves you". We were too busy telling people what they ought to believe to actually put those three little words into action. But the churches that actually did things; the churches that cared enough to get their hands dirty – they were the ones that people listened to.

'People should catch God's love, like a virus,' she continued. 'We should have been contagious with it, spreading it to whoever we came into contact with. Love seeps out and fills the air between us until you can't help but contract it.'

We walked out of the Self-Heal Unit, through thick plastic doors that swished open automatically. Beyond the unit was a corridor and then a large waiting room, where, for the first time, there was noise and bustle and activity. After the calm of the Self-Heal Unit, this was a world where real people were in real need. Here, at least, the world was busily caring. Nurses, dressed in blue and green plastic boiler-suits, rushed back and forth. Small, knee-high cleaning robots buzzed about sweeping and spraying disinfectant. Doctors strode past, apparently talking to thin air; until you looked closely and could see information flickering on their Putershades. The walls pulsed with light, which formed itself into posters for various events or campaigns; ante-natal classes, immunisation programmes, and one which said, 'Coral Snakes Are Dangerous! Citizens, Tread Carefully!'

'Thanks for the warning,' I muttered.

Despite the futuristic décor and devices, I could see many similarities to my time. Although they seemed to appear directly onto the wall, they were still the same kind of posters that adorned surgery and hospital waiting rooms in my day. The materials of the staff uniforms were different but the design remained resolutely traditional. There were even some dog-eared copies of *Which Pod* and *Cyberhome and Country* for people to look at while they waited. And there was still the unchanging atmosphere of a waiting room; the crying, the hushed words, the repressed pain.

We walked through the waiting room and out into the quiet sunshine of the late afternoon. There, Lydia's egg-pod moved silently through the air to pick us up.

'You know who built the hospitals?' she said, as the pod door began to shut. 'We did. The Christians, the churches, the monasteries. We built the first hospitals. It was Christians who first went into the slums and started treating people; Christians who started the first free education for all. Christians who changed conditions in prisons and factories and asylums. And we did it because when God walked in person on this earth he didn't just come and preach to people. He healed them. He fed them. He listened to their questions and their fears. He cared. He didn't give up on us as a lost cause. He wasn't like your suit. He didn't allow the fact that people were dead to get in the way of his cure.'

And with that, the pod hummed quietly away into the dusk.

Dear Miles,

You're right of course. Society has not changed that much in two thousand years. There is still oppression and injustice and poverty all around. On the surface, things may look different – indeed, things are different – but scratch the surface and you find the same fears and anxieties that were confronted by the first Christians all those years ago. I guess this is what Page encountered: hospital waiting rooms will always feel the same because they are full of the same fear and worry.

Whether there will be anyone to staff them is an interesting point raised by this episode. Page may be right in suggesting that the idea of 'vocation' is less frequently heard. In a world where more people went to church, more people would naturally have been exposed to the idea of loving their neighbour. Nowadays, I fear that we do not so much love our neighbour as invoice them for services rendered.

But I think that there is a bigger issue here, which has to do with our whole attitude to work. The Christian view of work was originally one of the things that distinguished them from the Greek culture around them. Greeks viewed work as a necessary evil and organised society so that most of it was done by slaves. There was nothing uplifting or spiritually enlightening about everyday work.

Christians in general – and Paul in particular – promoted a positive view of work, arguing that all Christians should do their work in a way that was honouring to their faith and their God.

Over the centuries, however, we have slipped back into a 'Greek' notion of work. It's not something that we like to think about. We would prefer to leave it to slaves – like the medi-suit in Page's story. As the years went by writers like Augustine, while not denigrating the ordinary working person, portrayed the religious or contemplative life as the higher calling. Only Christian work was a true vocation.

I recall in the porch of the church I used to attend a large map of the world. On this map, in various exotic locations, were pins, attached by lengths of wool to photos of various missionaries working in those parts of the world. We used to pray a lot for those missionaries. Yet there were people in our churches whose jobs were equally important. There were medical staff who saved lives on a regular basis; there were teachers and lawyers and nurses and builders and all manner of people engaged in vital tasks. Were they prayed for as regularly? I can't recall.

Perhaps you could put a map in your porch, with a picture of where everyone worked and lots of bits of wool. It would remind people that their work is a mission field, and their jobs are vocations and that God views them with every bit as much importance as he does people in 'Christian' work.

So, the early church had a more balanced view of work. They also had a deep commitment to the poor. As I said to you many letters ago, in its early years Christianity was marked by its emphasis on helping the poor and, throughout its history, there have been many examples of this in action. Indeed, those people who always sneer at Christianity for its intolerance and oppression would do well to look at the other side of the coin. As 'Lydia' says in the tale, Christianity was responsible for the first hospitals and schools. For example, Sunday schools were, originally, exactly that; they were places where children too poor to receive a proper education could be taught to read and write.

Many churches have played important roles in the regeneration of their community. Christians are working with asylum seekers, ethnic minorities, travellers, prostitutes, drug addicts – the many needy people in our society. It is important that the UK church retains this emphasis on working with the poor and fighting for their rights. On a global scale, one of the greatest triumphs of the church in recent years has been the Jubilee 2000 campaign.

So Christians always have been involved in social action; and they still are. Maybe the only point worth stating as a response to Page's account is to see the church's involvement as another sign to the world. It is important that the church retain this priority because it will act as a message to the world of what Christianity is all about. Social and community involvement, in this sense, becomes part of the church's outreach.

One of the great things about reaching out in this way is that it genuinely does deliver something that people want and need. And meaningful, relevant social-care projects challenge and undermine the stereotypes. If people are dismissive of the church's relevance to real life, then it becomes more important than ever for the church to demonstrate its faith, rather than merely talk about it. It becomes a vital part of the church's mission to get alongside the poor and the marginalised in our society and to show them that God cares for them.

I, more than anyone, know how immense the impact of Christian caring can be. The people who looked after Caroline, in the final days, were among the most 'Christian' people I have ever met. They were standing in a tradition of Christian care that has always been fundamental to the faith. They truly 'mourned with those who mourn' and if things have gone awry with my relationship with the church since then, they, at least, bear no part of the blame.

Best wishes,
Stephen

PS: One curious fact which might appeal to you. Caroline has a second cousin called Protheroe whose daughter has just joined the Royal Engineers. She is called, by a strange coincidence, Samantha. However, as far as I recall from seeing her at the funeral the girl definitely had two legs!

tHe set meNu 7

The large, brightly glowing sign out-
side the motel said 'Box-O-Rama Put-U-Up: Your Cube, The Way
You Want It'.

We walked into the reception where the glare was, if anything, even more striking. Only this time it was coming from the
bright yellow hair of the receptionist and her even brighter teeth.
It was like watching someone's head go super-nova.

'Hello, Citizens,' she grinned. 'How can I be of assistance?'

'Could you turn down your teeth please,' I muttered. 'They're
hurting my eyes.'

The receptionist looked at me in surprise, and then at Lydia.

'You must forgive my friend,' she said. 'He's old and dead,
and he has one leg too many.'

The receptionist shrugged. 'Whatever,' she said cheerfully
turning her grin up again to thermonuclear levels.

'We'd like two cubes please,' said Lydia.

'Certainly. Do you want large or extra-large futons?'

'Large.'

'What scent would you like?'

'I'm sorry?'

The receptionist looked at me. 'Your cube, Citizen. What scent would you like?'

I looked around me. 'This is a motel, right?' I asked. 'Surely all motel rooms smell the same. Slightly musty with a side-order of something unspeakable.'

'We'll take vanilla,' said Lydia hurriedly. 'With a touch of lemon.'

'Two lem-vanillas,' said the receptionist. 'And what colour would you like your cube?'

I was now completely bewildered.

'I can choose the colour?'

'Of course, Citizen,' said the receptionist. 'You can alter your environment how you wish. Your choice.'

I smiled grimly. This was a chance for revenge. 'I'll have yellow, then,' I said. 'With large purple spots.'

The smile didn't falter. 'As you wish. . . . Now, if you'll just swipe your IDs to register, please.'

'I'll handle that,' said Lydia, rather too hurriedly for my liking. She took the ID cards out of her pocket and casually waved them in front of the scanner. There was a beep and then two slim plastic cards slid out of a slot on the bottom of the scanner.

'Your rooms,' said the receptionist, handing Lydia the plastic door cards. 'You'll find your stack just down that corridor and straight through the glass doors.'

We walked out of reception, down a corridor, past a sign saying 'Knock-It-Back Alcobar – Where Happy Hour Lasts All Day', and through a pair of large, grubby double glass doors. Outside there was an open, airy courtyard, and straight ahead was a large structure which looked like an enormous stack of giant storage boxes.

'What is this place?'

'Cube-motel,' said Lydia, looking at our key cards to ascertain which cubes were ours. 'Just climb up to whichever cube is yours.'

The cubes were not, in fact, quite cubic. They were slightly longer than they were broad, with narrow openings at the front. They were constructed of a kind of off-white plastic and stacked five high and eight across. It was tupperware for humans; forty containers slotted together like lego; solitary confinement turned into a style statement.

'That's yours,' said Lydia, pointing upwards. 'At the top.'

'Ah,' I said. 'The receptionist's revenge.'

'We can change it if you like.'

'No, no, that's fine. See you in the morning.'

I began to climb the narrow stairs that zig-zagged up the side of the stacked boxes, leading out into a narrow metal landing that ran along the front of each floor.

Once I'd worked out how to use the card-key, I entered the room. It was eye-opening, in every sense. The walls were lemon yellow, and decorated with purple blobs, which changed and pulsated like huge, technicolor amoeba.

'Welcome to your room, Brigadier Protheroe,' breathed a soft, sensuous voice. 'We have prepared it entirely to your requirements. Do you have any other requirements?'

'No,' I said, with a sigh. 'Just leave me alone.'

'As you wish.'

I lay on the futon and breathed in the smell of lemon and vanilla, and tried not to think about my long, distinguished military career and the strange pain in my leg.

The next morning was fresh and bright and there was a smell of dew on the air. As I stood on the balcony outside my room, I could see London spread out before me – many of the landmarks were still in evidence, but the city was also studded with new buildings, tall, spindly, pointing into the sky with an arrogant grace.

I met Lydia at the breakfast table.

'Hello,' she said. 'How did you sleep?'

'Oh, the normal way. Just lay down and closed my eyes.'

'Good to know you're more cheerful this morning.'

'It's not my fault. I'm a one-legged female war-veteran trapped in a dead man's skin.'

I sat down at the table and felt the chair subtly mould itself beneath me.

'Why is it that all the furniture keeps changing around here?' I asked. 'Why can't a chair just be a chair?'

'You just wait,' said Lydia, with a mischievous glint in her eye. 'Let's eat, shall we? Menu,' she said, and the surface of the table shimmered and then was suddenly full of writing – hundreds of words flowing like liquid spilt across the surface.

'That's not a menu,' I said in bewilderment. 'That's a novel.'

'It's customer choice,' said Lydia. 'People don't all want the same thing.' She paused again. 'Kippers,' she said.

I stared at her. 'Kippers?' I asked.

'I was ordering breakfast,' she explained.

'Oh.' I looked around me for the waiter, but no-one was there. 'Who from?'

'The table of course.'

'Of course. Stupid of me.' I looked down at the table. It looked, unusually for a piece of furniture, slightly smug.

'Hallo, Brigadier Protheroe,' it chirruped. 'Or can I call you Samantha?'

'No, you can't.'

'Oh. Well, my name is Table 14, and I'll be your table this morning.'

'Oh goody,' I said, without bothering to hide the sarcasm in my voice. 'You're learniture aren't you?'

'Not quite,' explained the table cheerfully. 'Learniture is a different branch of the Intelligent Furniture Sector. We are Serviture; furniture which just loves to serve. Our job is to make sure that all your needs are catered for. Which reminds me, can I interest you in our special Germo-Fibre pancakes with added bran? To help you with your . . . er . . . problem.'

There was a rather strained silence. 'What problem?' I asked.

The table's mechanical voice dropped to what it obviously considered to be a confidential whisper. 'Well, between you and me, Citizen, reports came from your bathroom that you're not what you might call regular.'

'Reports from my bathroom?' I looked at Lydia accusingly. 'Who's been spying on me in the bathroom?'

'I received the data from your lavatory seat, of course. It's interactive.'

'An interactive lavatory seat?'

'Of course. Serviture working for your own health and safety Citizen.' The table gleamed proudly. 'Oh, and we had further confirmation from your medi-suit's health data profile, posted yesterday, twenty-one-oh-six hours. It sounds to me like you need Germo-Fibre, the world's most popular roughage substitute.'

I turned to Lydia. 'This is worse than a police state! It's a police state that spies on you and then tries to sell you things.' I exclaimed. 'Is there no escape?'

'Not really,' she said, with an amused shrug. 'It's the national datanet. It's linked to health, banks, shopping centres, CCTV screens, car registration scanners, any electronic device really. It was introduced in your day, actually, under the guise of an anti-terrorist measure. But then the government started linking more and more electronic surveillance together, and that led to spiralling costs. So they opened it up to private sponsors as well. The net result is that you're never far away from a sales pitch. We've just sort of got used to it.'

'So, can I put you down for the roughage?' asked the table.

'No you cannot,' I snapped. 'I'll have a croissant.'

The table beeped. 'Of course. I have sixteen different kinds of croissant, Citizen. Do you want chocolate, all butter, almond . . .'

'Just a plain one please.'

'Plain,' sniffed the table. 'Not much of a challenge there, is there?' There was a pause. 'What kind of jam do you want with your croissant?' it asked hopefully. 'We've got apricotmarmaladeraspberrystrawberryblackcurrantpeachplum −'

'No jam.' I said hurriedly. 'I just want a plain croissant. And a strong coffee.'

There was an ominous pause.

'What kind of coffee?' enquired the table. 'I have thirty-eight different kinds. I'll list them for you −'

I leant close to the surface of the table. 'I wouldn't do that, if I were you,' I whispered. 'Otherwise I might be forced to polish you. With an axe.'

'You see?' said the table, sounding rather aggrieved. 'This is exactly what happens if you don't eat properly. You get all bunged up and full of . . .'

There was an ominous pause.

'Rage,' concluded the table.

'Please,' I said, wearily, 'just a croissant. Or I will get some sandpaper and show you what roughage really means.'

'I'm only giving you a choice . . . ,' it said, sounding hurt.

'Just a strong black coffee,' I hissed. 'And make it fast.'

The table shimmered and went black.

'Someone got out of the wrong side of their cube this morning,' said Lydia.

'I can't cope with all this choice being flung at me. And I don't want lavatory seats and medical suits reporting on my health problems, thank you very much.'

'It's only doing its job. It's the way it was programmed; it has to try to get some idea of what you want,' said Lydia. 'Admittedly it's doing it in an annoying and intrusive way, but at least it's trying.'

'So that's a good thing, is it?' I snarled. 'Thirty-eight kinds of coffee and a talking toilet seat is the height of customer service?' I looked down at the table, which seemed to be sulking. 'The kind of hotels I used to go to you had two choices of breakfast: foul or uneatable.'

'Yes,' said Lydia. 'The set menu. You had it everywhere. And nowhere more than in your churches.'

'Oh, here we go ...,' I muttered. 'I hear the sound of a metaphor crashing through the undergrowth. This is the point where you tell me everything we ever did was wrong.'

'Not everything,' she said. 'But you did more or less the same thing for everybody.'

Suddenly the middle of the table slid open and from inside the tube came two coffees and the rest of our breakfast. Lydia took a coffee and sipped it. 'Just as I ordered,' she sighed. 'Thank you Table 14.'

'Thank you, Citizen,' chirped the table.

I took my coffee. It did smell rather good actually. And the croissant was wonderful; a billowing curve of buttery pastry. I inhaled in the aroma. The table seemed to be waiting for something.

'What's those two little words, you've forgotten?' it said to me.

'Fire wood,' I replied, and it suddenly shut down with a 'hmph.'

Lydia smiled at me. We ate our breakfast, and for a moment, I almost felt like apologising to the table. However, I was rescued just in time by Lydia saying, 'You know what the four most useless words of your time were? "One size fits all".' She paused. 'What that invariably meant was that it looked bad on everybody. You saw that on an item and you knew that everyone would be able to put it on, but no-one would enjoy wearing it. It was a cheap and easy – and often lazy – way of doing things. And the church did exactly the same thing.'

She leaned back and sipped her coffee.

'Think about church services in your day. Weren't they "one size fits all"? Oh yes, some had louder songs than others, some had longer sermons, some were led by men, some by women, and some by men dressed as women; but they were all more or less the same. And what that meant was that there were loads of people who were excluded from church simply because they didn't like church. It wasn't that they didn't love God, you understand. It was simply that they didn't like the way that we talked about him.'

'I know all this. I talked about it a lot.'

'Yes,' she said. 'You were good at talking . . .'

'What's that supposed to mean?'

She didn't answer. Instead she reached down into her bright silver coat and pulled out a book. She flipped it across the table; an old paperback, its pages brittle and yellowed with age.

'*Small is Beautiful*,' I read. 'I used to have a copy like this.'

'That *was* your copy. Look.'

I opened the book and looked at the flyleaf. There, scrawled on the yellow paper, was my name.

'Where did you get this?'

'I bought it from your estate. After your death. It was one of the few books that weren't ruined by ... by what happened ...'

'What do you mean? What did happen? And how did my books get ruined? Has this anything to do with the water-buffalo?'

She shook her head. 'That doesn't matter now. The point is the title is right: small is beautiful. But you lot always believed it to be ugly.' She sighed. 'The church of your time was locked into numbers, locked into a church structure which meant large numbers of people meeting to do things in the same way. So when the numbers fell away it became depressing, because you were still trying to act in a way that needed lots of people.'

'I don't understand.'

'It's quite simple. You need twenty-two people to play a football match. If twelve or even ten people turn up you can still put on a game of sorts. But if only two people turn up, you'd do far better to have a game of tennis.' She smiled. 'One of the problems with the church in your time was that it carried on staging football matches when it should have been encouraging everyone to try their hand at tennis.'

I stared at her. 'Are you sure that's just coffee you're drinking?'

'I know it's early in the morning,' she said, 'but do try to think. The point is that small can be beautiful, providing it's not trying to be big. You have to do church differently with small numbers, but you can still do it. And successfully too.' She pointed at her coffee. 'I like espressos,' she said. 'Small, but incredibly potent. If you ever get back, tell your people to stop trying to be cappuccinos and try to be more like espressos.'

'I'm sure they'll be pleased to hear that. And they say the church is too middle-class . . .'

'Small groups,' she said, ignoring me. 'They could have changed everything, if you'd really believed in them. If you'd seen them as opportunities rather than as an admission of defeat.'

'You're talking about cell churches.'

'I'm talking about lots and lots of different kinds of churches. Different flavours. All concentrating on the same things, but doing it in different ways. We built an entire system based on persuading people to come into a big old building, sit down and listen. And it stopped working some time in the 1950s. Maybe we should have gone and listened to them.'

'So how do you do that?'

'You ask people. You get feedback from them. You find out what they want to know about and how they want it to be taught. You create services to do different things at different times.'

'You mean cell church.'

'Yes, as long as cells don't become prisons. As long as there is always room for development and for people to change. You see, what small groups can do really well, is create community. They enable real relationships and real commitment to one another in a way that huge megachurches never can. They are church and community at a more accessible, more appropriate scale. She picked up a piece of toast and bit into it.

'Bite-sized,' she mumbled, her mouth full of bread. 'If you like.'

The table beeped.

'I was just wondering, if you'd like to choose from our selection of 340 low-calorie lunches, Citizen,' it said.

'Of course,' said Lydia. 'There's such a thing as too much choice . . .'

→•←

After breakfast, we checked out of the hotel and walked down to where the egg-pods were waiting.

Across the road was an old school – possibly dating back to Victorian times. Through the gates, children were filing, their laughter, shouts and general chaos the same as I was used to, and the same, no doubt, as every school child has made, throughout history.

'Some things stay on,' I said, pointing at the school. 'Some buildings haven't been replaced.'

'You haven't seen inside,' said Lydia, pressing her finger on the fingerprint identification plate that operated the egg-pod. 'It's a different world in there now. All Virtuality education and interactive teaching. The building may be Victorian, but the teaching methods are thoroughly mid twenty-first century.'

'Which reminds me,' I said, climbing into the pod, 'all that you were saying about choice and change and all that. I'm all for that, but what about the quality issues?'

'Quality?'

'Yes. What about worship? What about teaching? How can you ensure that people are taught well in groups?'

Lydia started to laugh. It started as a chuckle and then spread throughout her body, until she was sobbing with mirth. I just stared at her. This wasn't the repressed, severe woman I had come to know.

'You are too much, really you are!' she exclaimed. 'If I didn't know what you'd written, what you'd said . . . well, sometimes you just amaze me.'

'I don't see what's so funny,' I said haughtily.

'Can't you hear yourself?' she asked. 'Asking about the quality of teaching? Are you really trying to tell me that every church in the country taught their people so brilliantly?'

I looked at her. 'You may have a point there.'

She wiped her eyes and looked across to the school, where the last of the children were racing in to beat the clock.

'Look, the fact is that so many people were put off church because there was simply no variety in how it was done. Take worship, for example. Worship is so much more than we made it. We limited it to singing songs while a few people banged away on guitars, but who defines what worship is? And as for teaching – wherever we went we received the same messages in the same ways. But that's not how Jesus taught. Sometimes he preached. Sometimes he led discussion groups. Sometimes he just told stories. Sometimes he just did things and left people to draw their own conclusions. So why did we assume that one person talking to a room full of other people was the best way to teach?

'Small groups allow you to teach at their pace. Each Sunday morning we would expect a large number of customers to come in, sit down and receive huge portions of whatever food we chose to give them. And then we wondered why some people got terminal cases of spiritual indigestion. But if we'd actually *listened* to them, we might have found out that they were interested in our cooking – just in different portions and with a few more dishes.'

'But what about unity?' I asked. 'What about the idea of one church?'

'It's a mirage,' she said. 'Always has been. Since when has there ever been "one church" in the sense that you're talking about? I mean, when was there an occasion where there was just one church in any town or city or village? From the Middle Ages onwards, there have always been alternative ways of doing church. Our unity – such as it is – has never been in one big meeting in one big building. It's been in Christ himself. Unity in diversity and all that.'

'So you're saying that we should just turn everything into cell churches.'

'You already have them,' she replied. 'The average weekly attendance of churches in your time was around fifty-five people. That's the average. So there were hundreds and hundreds of churches with far fewer than that. And all these churches – the ones that were struggling on with fewer than twenty people in them – they already were cell churches. But even then they carried on acting in the same way. They carried on playing football, when they could have had a great time playing tennis.'

Suddenly she looked sad.

'We failed so badly to listen to people, especially young people. They wanted a church that allowed them to express themselves. Not one that made them sit in rows and listen all the time. They wanted a church that offered variety, but we made them sit through the same thing again and again until they got bored. They wanted a church that involved them – gave them tasks and challenges. We pushed them to one side and told them to conform. We carried on serving up the same food in the same way and never changing the menu. And we wondered why so many customers went elsewhere.' She stared at me. 'When you go back, tell them to give church back to the people. Before it's too late.'

Dear Miles,

You are too young to remember this, but there used to be a time when you could go into a shoe shop and find the same styles there as on your last visit. There used to be a time when the packaging of goods didn't constantly change, when you could actually get things repaired. There used to be a time when there was less change.

These days, however, we live at the opposite extreme. We are a nation of neophiles; constantly searching for, and embracing the new. New products, new experiences, new activities; in the consumer world that is western society, we worship the new. Change is not only good, it is a god.

The church, on the other hand, is neophobic; it is allergic to newness. Part of this is because any organisation, once it gets over a certain size, prefers standardisation to innovation. As organisations tend to bureaucracies, so they tend to neophobia, because the one thing a bureaucrat can't stand is change. It always generates so much paperwork.

The other main reason that the churches do more or less the same thing, is because they believe in permanence as a virtue. The main elements of a service – Communion, worship, preaching, liturgy, etc. – have been set in stone for centuries, although different traditions emphasise different elements. The traditions of the church are seen as sacred in themselves; change them and you tamper with the very essence of what church is.

So, here you have the very essence of a conflict. And it explains why so many Christians – particularly those of a younger vintage – feel such antipathy towards church. They are neophiles stuck in a neophobic church. They crave variety and newness, yet every Sunday they go to a place that is substantially the same. They might appreciate the permanence of some of the church's structures and activities; but they are also desperate for change. To put it in layman's terms, they're bored.

I felt this strongly reading the latest episode from Page's travels. He exhibits all the symptoms of a neophile, albeit a somewhat reluctant one. He wants change, but not too much change. He wants things to be different, and yet there is a part of him which wants things to remain the same. He is trapped between a neophile society and a neophobic church.

Yet it need not be such a tension. It is perfectly possible to adhere to the traditional elements of a church service without having to bore the congregation to death. All you have to do is make sure you distinguish between form and function.

For example, the church habitually believes the terms 'teaching' and 'preaching' are interchangeable. In virtually every church when we come to a time of teaching it means a man (and it usually is a man) standing and speaking. We have sanctified the sermon. Preaching has become the 'holy' way for teaching to take place in the church.

The result is that we have what I call 'Eutychus Congregations'. You'll remember that story in Acts 20. During Paul's final visit to Troas he is speaking to some Christians in a room on the third floor of a house (sounds like a cell group to me). With the heat from the lamps,

Eutychus, a young man sitting by the window, falls asleep, tumbles out of the window and is killed. He literally died of boredom. (The story, of course, ends happily when the boy is restored to life. After which Paul goes on talking, until dawn.) Nevertheless, the country is now full of Eutychus congregations, where, as the speaker drones on and on, people are dying of boredom, falling out of the building, and never coming back.

I'm not against preaching *per se* – few things are more inspiring, electrifying or potentially life-changing than a good sermon – but we have to recognise that, outside the church, most people don't learn this way. Every day, thousands of the people in our congregations go on courses or engage in training. Young or old, in work or at school, they're learning all the time. And hardly any of them are learning by having someone speak at them at length. Instead modern, secular training and education uses a huge variety of teaching techniques – especially techniques which involve hands on activities and which encourage questions and discussion.

The fact is that the early church, coming as it did from the Jewish culture, probably had more discussions than anything else. Jesus' teaching provoked questions and debate. When he wanted his disciples to learn something he sent them out on work experience.

Take the passage in Acts that I quoted above. The two Greek words used to describe what Paul was doing are *dialegomai* and *homileo*. Both really mean to converse with, to discuss, to engage in a dialogue. In other words, Paul wasn't preaching. He was talking with the people in that room, not talking at them. Which is not to say that he *wasn't* boring, but at least he was engaging in a long, boring debate, not delivering a long, boring sermon.

So, teaching need not be preaching. Worship need not be hymns or modern worship songs. Prayer need not be one person talking to God at the front while the rest of us try to keep up. All the traditional elements of the church service can be reinterpreted and reinvented for our different cultures.

Having said all that, one of the main problems with Page's picture of the future is that it fails to recognise the changes that are already being made in the present. This is understandable – if you are staring into the distance, it's hard to see what is right in front of your eyes – but the fact is that there are many different radical experiments with church going on at the moment. There is a lot of experimentation with worship, using everything from labyrinths to light shows.

And there are new models of church which, I believe, offer a lot of scope for combating the kind of problems Page raises here. I will just briefly mention three of the most popular models; not, of course, the only models available, but they do appear to be the most popular.

The Cell Church

Cell church is a concept which has spread throughout the world. A cell church is a small group of believers who meet regularly for worship, normally in houses. The main difference between a cell church and a house group is the attitude. For a cell church congregation, this *is* their church. There is also a level of autonomy and accountability that is different from a house group. Cell churches are mission-oriented. They exist to multiply.

Some cells exist entirely as a network, independent of a big congregation. Others are linked into, and supported by, a big, main congregation. In the latter model, the various cells in an area will get together for worship services every so often, but the focus of all their teaching and worship remains the cell.

I suppose I warm to this model because it is clearly found in the early church. All early churches were cell groups, because they all met in homes. In the very largest houses, the maximum congregation would have been forty or fifty; in most houses there would have been room for twelve at most. (Indeed, some experts believe that the Christians in a particular city rarely if ever met *en masse*. Not only would there not have been buildings big enough to hold them all, it would have been very dangerous to do so.)

Cell churches encourage intimacy and sharing. Their teaching style is discursive, individual needs and problems can be addressed, and there is a wide scope for creativity and flexibility in worship. Perhaps the most significant reason, though, for the UK church to adopt the cell approach is because most UK churches already *are* cell churches; they already are small congregations. I can't help feeling that if they recognised this fact, they might feel slightly better about life.

The Network Church

The network church is church based, not on geographical boundaries, but on one or more 'networks'. These networks might be based in the workplace, or by age or gender, or by leisure interests or social grouping. Accordingly, network churches do not base themselves in church buildings; they can be found in offices, sports clubs, health clubs, pubs – anywhere where there is a network of relationships. (I don't want to bang the early church drum again, but this may well have been a model familiar to that era, with churches based around trade guilds.)

Many network churches have grown out of frustration with the present set up, in particular with the way that the ordinary traditional structures do not fit in with the lives of many younger people today. The network church simply offers a better 'fit' with their lifestyles.

If the parish system is a kind of horizontal grid across the land, network church is a vertical church; it breaks the boundaries of the parish but roots itself in something which is often much more relevant to people's lives; their work and social relationships, which in many cases is a much more real landscape in which they can express their faith.

The Minster Model

This name *minster* comes from the Latin for monastery (*monasterium*, if you must know). In Anglo-Saxon times the minster was a large church, which was the centre of a vast 'mega-parish'. The minster was staffed by groups of clergy living in community, who would be sent out to found new churches, and make converts. The minster church was the way in which pagan Britain was first evangelised in Celtic times. Many churches and cathedrals are still designated 'minsters', including the cathedrals of York, Lincoln, Ripon, Southwell and Lichfield and churches such as Beverley and Wimborne. Given the level of church planting being engaged in by these churches, one has to wonder whether they should be sued under the trades description act.

Nowadays, the minster model is a model of church based on mission springing from a central core. Minster churches are large, well-resourced mother churches which send missioners out, or which take satellite churches under their wing. Significantly, churches operating the minster model often use both cells and network churches. In one major church in the north of England which operates on this model, a network of small clusters meet regularly. Each cluster is linked into one of the various celebrations of the church. And the clusters are not merely geographical, they are also based around themes (such as contemporary life issues or relating faith to the workplace) or social networks (such as those struggling with addiction, those who need a cluster during the day).

The minster model provides a way for the big churches to share their resources without having to draw everyone in to the centre. It is an attempt to combine the power of a big church with the intimacy of the small community group and to offer a wide range of worship styles to suit all tastes.

Obviously, Miles, there are more models than this, and many different variants on these models. There are many 'classic' churches which are retaining their structure while experimenting with new forms of worship and engaging with today's culture in new ways. However, I do think that these three styles of church will be the dominant models of the future. There will be small, intimate, intentionally accountable groups in homes and buildings throughout the UK; there will be churches built around relationships and different social groupings; and there will be some – if only a handful – of megachurches, spreading their resources around a wider geographical region.

What these models all have in common is a sense of mission. The church of the future must be a missionary church, for it has no other choice. At the moment, many churches prefer to look after their own before going out and finding some more, but if it keeps to this practice, there will not, in the end, be anyone left to pastor.

The church of the future will be a missionary church or it will be a dead church. It can choose which model to structure itself on, but when it comes to mission, there will be no choice at all.

Best wishes,
Stephen

liFe's a BeAch 8

Something had been nagging me about this new world. Many things had looked the same, only with new bits bolted on. Hotels were still hotels, they were just stackable and built out of plastic. The houses still looked like houses, the shops still were recognisably shops. But something was wrong. Something was missing.

Then I realised what it was: people. There were hardly any people on the streets. The egg-pod slipped silently through places that were half-empty. Oh, there were people out and about, but nothing to the numbers that used to throng to London.

I looked around me. 'Not many people about . . . ,' I ventured.

'No,' replied Lydia. 'That's the congestion charge for you.'

'Er . . . I thought that was vehicles.'

'It used to be vehicles,' she agreed, 'but then it got gradually widened. Bicycles first. Then all forms of wheeled transport. Pushchairs; wheelie bins; those little shopping trolleys that old ladies wheel about. And still the place was incredibly crowded. So in the end – about ten years ago – they introduced a charge for pedestrians.'

'Well, that seems to have done the trick.'

'Yes,' said Lydia. 'Of course, what's helped is the rollout of the Putershades and the advances they've made in Virtuality. There's not so much need to physically go places any more.'

'Virtuality?' I asked. 'Is that like the virtual reality we used to have?'

'Virtuality bears the same relationship to your virtual reality as . . .' She thought for a moment. 'As a high-turbo twin-engined jetboat does to a canoe. It's the same basic content, but –'

'Faster.'

'Faster. Bigger. Brighter. More powerful. More exciting. Generally better in every way.'

She reached into a pocket and took out a pair of black sunglasses.

'Virtuality,' she repeated. 'Anywhere you want to be you can be without having to leave your own space. And it's a synthophysical experience – you smell it, feel it, experience it in every detail. It's all delivered over the Ultranet.'

'You mean the Internet.'

She laughed. 'You are *so* 2010,' she said. 'The Ultranet. It's . . . er . . . a bit bigger than the Internet.'

'We're talking turbo-powered jetboats again are we?'

'We're talking turbo-powered ocean liners. It's . . . oh, I can't explain. You have to see it for yourself. Here.' She handed me a pair of black sunglasses. 'Putershades,' she explained. 'Put them on.'

Gingerly, I put them on. They were just dark glasses, although I couldn't help noticing a small, green light that blinked on and off in the lower left-hand corner of my vision.

'What do I do?'

'Boot up.'

'Pardon?'

'Say "Ultranet",' she instructed.

'Er . . . Ultranet,' I ventured.

A voice said, 'Loading . . . please wait.'

And then the world started to cave in.

The world I could see through my sunglasses – Lydia, the streets, the inside of the egg-pod – began to dissolve, to melt. Lights and numbers began to flash in front of my eyes; great whirling balls of colour flipped and pulsed across the screen. Then I started to fall through the lights, like falling through multicoloured clouds. I knew that in the real world, in the physical me-and-Lydia world, I was sitting still; but at the same time I knew I was falling, and that far below me, and advancing at enormous speed, was what looked like a city. It rushed towards me. I was free-falling into the void. Panicking slightly, I tore the glasses from my face.

'Wow,' I said, shakily. 'Wow.'

'It's always like that the first time,' said Lydia.

'You could have warned me.'

'Maybe,' she shrugged, showing an almost complete lack of sympathy. 'But there's not much that can prepare you for it, really. We've just got used to it.' She made an attempt to sound more concerned. 'You don't get hurt or anything,' she said. 'You just land in the cityscape.'

I shook my head, which was still dizzy with vertigo and coloured lights. 'The last time I saw anything like this was at a Pink Floyd concert.'

Lydia drew in her breath sharply. 'You saw Pink Floyd?' she asked, in a hushed voice. 'For real?'

I did a double-take. I'd impressed Lydia.

'Well, yes,' I said. 'But you always came out of a Floyd gig humming the light show. They were that kind of band.'

'Pink Floyd ...' she said, in an awe-filled voice. 'I keep forgetting how you're from the past.' A thought suddenly occurred to her. 'Did you ever see Yes? I've got *Tales from Topographic Oceans* on the mp3-juke somewhere ...'

Hurriedly I grabbed the glasses. 'I think I'm ready to have another go,' I said, putting the glasses back on. I'd rather free-fall than listen to Yes. Whatever was waiting for me, it couldn't be worse than prog-rock.

Again there was the vertigo-inducing light show and the odd sensation of falling and once again the ground started to hurtle towards me. Below me was a city, stretching out in every direction; houses, streets, trees, plants ... an entire cityscape on the lenses of a pair of sunglasses. And me about to crash into it. I braced myself for impact and, just as I reached it, the whole world seemed to flip; or maybe I flipped; and I stopped. I was not standing on the streets, I was hovering just above the city, with it stretched out below me.

'Can you see the City yet?' asked Lydia. Her voice sounded distant, even though she was sitting next to me.

'I can see it ... it's vast.'

'It's just a way of navigating around. A way of organising all the information that's out there. You can wander the streets at random and see what's out there, or you can tell it where you want to go.'

'So what do I do? Just speak?' As I spoke the words I could see them flow across the bottom of the Putershades, liquid, moving characters of pale green light.

'Speak.'

'Okay,' I said, 'Take me to a beach in Bermuda.'

There was a click and a pause. Everything went dark. Then – and this is what hit me first – I could *smell* the sea. I could smell the salty ozone tang, and I could hear gulls in the distance. Suddenly it was as if someone had turned on a huge light, and I found myself standing – literally standing – on a beach. I wasn't just looking at it, I was *there*.

'This is incredible,' I said. 'I'm really in Bermuda.'

'No,' said a voice from far away. 'No, you're not. You just think you're in Bermuda. Your brain is just being fooled.'

'But how? I can smell it.' I wiggled my feet. 'I can feel the warm sand beneath my feet.'

'The arms of the glasses have tiny electrodes which break the skin behind your ears,' said Lydia's distant voice. 'They're feeding neuro-electrical impulses into your brain. That part of your brain which deals with touch and smell and all those other senses is being over-ridden by the data from the Putershades. Your brain is convinced that you're there, and it's mimicking the physical sensations. You think, therefore you sunbathe.'

I looked around me. It was a beautiful sight. The sea was turquoise, with the sunlight sparkling on it like diamonds. The coconut-laden palm trees waved gently in the wind. The white sand stretched away before me. I looked further; in the distance, stretching into the sea, was a rocky outcrop that seemed naggingly familiar. Then I realised.

'Lydia,' I said. 'You'll never believe this, but there's a pile of rocks here that look just like the McDonald's logo.'

'Subliminal advertising,' she replied. 'Try looking at the coconuts.'

I did. Each coconut had 'Sponsored by Bounty' printed on the side. Underneath the palm trees, standing drinking at a beach bar were people, people who were waving to me. They were tanned and attractive, dressed in bright Bermuda shorts and bathing costumes, hair bleached blonde by the sunshine; they were loudly and obviously having fun. 'Hi there!' I could hear them call. 'Come and join us for the refreshing taste of Bacardi!' And then, suddenly, the whole beach juddered, and half of the sea seemed to go a funny colour and slide out of the side of the screen.

'What's happening?' I asked.

'We are sorry,' said a gentle, calming voice, 'we are having problems connecting to *bermudaworld-dot-beach*. In the meantime, here is some music.' Twanging guitar music started to filter into the back of my brain. It sounded worryingly like Yes. 'We have selected some music to reflect your interests, as recorded in recent conversations,' said the voice. Quickly, I took the specs off and the beach disappeared, to be replaced by the quiet, empty London streets.

Strangely my return to the real world left me feeling rather sad and empty. It was an aching, bleak, end-of-holiday feeling, for I had been on the beach, feeling the sun, smelling the sea. It felt so real; and now reality felt so much less fun.

Lydia looked at me. 'Now you know why so many people spend all their time in Virtuality. It's so much nicer than the real thing. And the coming out can be ... difficult.' She gestured at the empty streets. 'So an increasing number of people spend their time scoring Virtuality. It's a world on drugs. In homes, in offices, or in the vast Virtuality bars, we have a society of people dosed up on unreality, scoring on the artificial, the temporary. It's a drug; an addictive, pleasurable, ultimately destructive pleasure.'

'I see,' I said. But I wasn't really listening. Something inside me was urging me to put the Putershades back on, to visit another beach, or fly to another country, or speak to some of the inhabitants. I wanted to mingle again with those people on the beach; to swim in the sea or sip a Bacardi. I shook my head and fought off the feeling. I had not come all this way to take refuge in unreality. And anyway, I reminded myself, it's not real.

'Don't people mind that it's not real?' I asked Lydia. 'Or,' I added, remembering the logos on the beach and the not-so-subtle product placement, 'that it's full of people trying to sell them things?'

'Well, the problem is a bit more complicated than that,' replied Lydia. 'The thing is that after a while it does become "real". For many of our citizens, this *is* reality. And as for the advertising, well, when you live in a consumer culture – and accept that that is the only culture worth having – of course people will sell you things. It goes with the territory. Originally there was a big outcry and many promises to keep the Ultranet free of all commercial influences. But you can't hold back forces of that sort. In the end the money was too alluring. Now . . .' She shook her head. 'Well, I don't think anyone ever notices any more.'

'The FA Cup,' I murmured.

'I'm sorry?'

'It's just that in, I think, the early nineties, the Football Association declared that the FA Cup would never be tainted by sponsorship. But by the end of the decade it was sponsored – and nobody questioned it. We just accepted it as part of the norm.'

'Exactly.'

'But don't people get bored?'

'Oh no. There are always new places to visit, new sites to see. There are always newer, more potent Ultranet-driven experiences just waiting down the line. Consumerism is based on the idea of permanent dissatisfaction, of keeping people always wanting more. They keep people online with their promises of greater things just around the corner. And you can convince people that to live that way, to live always craving the new experience or the latest product, is the way to live.' She smiled, but she was not amused. 'You know, if you sugar the pills heavily enough, then people will never notice that they're overdosing.'

'But hasn't the Ultranet brought some good things as well? I remember the Internet being a wonderful thing. All the knowledge on line. All the convenience, the communication.'

'All the pornography and the spam mail and the chatroom perverts,' said Lydia.

'Oh, well, if you want to pick out the bad bits,' I replied. 'I mean, every technology always has those who abuse it. As soon as any new medium of communication is invented, someone comes along and uses it for immoral purposes. The caveman who made the first cave paintings painted horses and bison and deer. But you can bet it was only a matter of days before another caveman came along and painted a picture of Miss Neanderthal without her fur clothes on. And he probably charged entrance as well. All communication is used for bad things as well as good. But that doesn't make the technology itself wrong.'

'No,' agreed Lydia, 'but all technology changes us. We shape our tools, and then our tools shape us. There was nothing wrong with the Internet in itself. Just as there's nothing wrong with the Ultranet in our time. But they have shaped people's consciousness. They change the way we react to each other. And few people have the strength to walk away from them and see them for what they really are.'

'Meaning?'

'Is a chatroom really a substitute for a real chat? Is the ability to interact with people the other side of the world really better than the ability to love your neighbour?'

I waved at her dismissively. 'I've heard all these objections. They aren't wrong ways of communicating. They're just different ways of communicating.'

'Well, maybe we've drifted off the point a bit,' she said. 'And maybe we haven't. The point is, I guess, that both in your time and now there are people whose lives are spent in different places and different realities. If the church claims to have what's true – what's *really* real – then it has to go and find these people.' She gave me a look which indicated that the conversation was at an end. 'Put your Putershades back on,' she ordered. She reached into a compartment at the front of the egg-pod and drew out another pair of glasses. 'We're going on a little journey.'

'To Bermuda?' I said hopefully.

'No. To the jungle.' She lifted a flap on the front of her silver cybernated suit and said 'Jungle story, please.'

The suit beeped. And then, from somewhere on the front of her suit – I didn't like to look at exactly *where* – a slightly tinny voice spoke. 'Destination ready,' it said. She looked at me and noticed I was blushing. 'What's the matter?'

'Er . . . it's just all these voices and talking objects. Your left . . . um . . . "chest" just spoke to you.'

She snorted.

'It's only a built in speaker,' she said. 'It's here,' she pointed.

'I know where it is, thank you,' I said, hurriedly. 'I just don't know why they had to put it there.'

'Oh that's nothing,' she said. 'You should see where they've put the printer.'

I was lost for words.

'Put your Putershades on,' she repeated.

With the sunglasses on, the voice that had sounded so tinny as it emerged from Lydia's . . . er . . . 'speakers', sounded bassier and boomier. After the same, disorientating free-fall into the Ultranet, we were standing on a grey, plain street. I was aware of Lydia standing next to me, only this was not Lydia as she was in real life. This was a younger Lydia, a Lydia with the wrinkles smoothed out. She seemed sort of blurry.

'You're looking different,' I said. 'Have you done something to your hair?'

'It's a Botox filter,' explained Lydia.

'A what?'

'A Botox filter. A visual filter that takes your real appearance and smoothes it out. The Ultranet does it automatically. It's sponsored by a face cream manufacturer. They take your basic database profile and subtly improve it.'

'Ah. Well, it suits you. You're looking good.'

'You don't look so bad yourself. I particularly like the medals.'

I looked down and for the first time I was aware of my own body – or at least the way it was being represented in this strange realm. I was wearing a brigadier's outfit of military green, and I had a large number of medal ribbons attached to my chest. There were a lot of medals, but then there seemed to be a lot of room for them. Rather alarmingly I now appeared to have a chest big enough, not only for one of Lydia's speakers but also for a full surround-sound system. With extra large sub-woofers.

'I don't believe it . . .' I muttered. 'No-one can be this shape. At least, not without a lot of scaffolding and the help of a competent welder.'

'It's just another filter,' explained Lydia. 'It looks like Brigadier Protheroe paid to have the Ultranet apply an Enhancement Macro. It's a programme that, well, emphasises your best qualities, shall we say.'

I thought for a moment. 'So people pay to have these filters applied?' I asked. 'I thought you said they were automatically added?' I looked at her. Her Botox-filtered, wrinkle-free face was blushing.

'Well,' she mumbled. 'A person wants to look their best.'

'Oh Lydia,' I said, in mock-serious tones. 'I never thought that you would be so vain.'

'Oh shut up,' she said. 'Let's move on, shall we?' She looked around her. 'Jungle narrative,' she snapped.

Suddenly the street faded from view, and everything went very dark.

'Beginning narrative,' said a fluting, musical voice. The darkness seemed to thicken slightly, to solidify. I suddenly began to feel hot, and a thin bead of sweat began to trickle down the back of my uniform. Then shards of light began to appear, falling down to the ground like autumn leaves and gradually forming themselves into puddles of light around my feet. I could now see deep, dappled shadows all around me, branches brushing my face, dense vegetation beneath my feet. There were animal noises; birdsong and the buzzing of insects. I was in a jungle. A hot jungle. A hot, dark jungle.

'There was once a village in the jungle,' said the voice. Suddenly the branches swept aside and there it was. We moved through the leaves, into a clearing, and there, dim and darkened, was a collection of rudimentary huts.

'The jungle was very dense and dark and the people in the village never saw much sunlight,' continued the voice. 'Most days they would light their torches in the afternoon, and they lived their lives in gloom. Every now and then, they would hear the wind rustling the treetops and they would look up, uncertainly, and wonder what was happening above them. They thought that something must be happening, but they could not see it. Occasionally, the sunlight filtered through the leaves of the trees and reached down piercing the gloom. When this happened, the villagers were very happy and they danced in the sunlight. But these moments were rare: mostly it was dark and cold and gloomy.'

As the computer, or the sunglasses, or whoever it was narrated this tale, the Virtuality images reflected the narrative. Villagers lit torches, looked around gloomily, gathered excitedly around small patches of sunlight that had somehow found their way onto the forest floor.

'One day,' continued the storyteller, 'a stranger appeared in the village.'

And then a man appeared among them. Taller than they were. His colouring darker than their shadowy, pale skin.

'Where did you come from?' the villagers asked him.

He pointed. 'From up there,' he said. 'From the tops of the trees, where the air is fresh and the wind blows in your face and the birds sing.'

The villagers looked amazed.

'There is an "up there"?' they asked.

'Oh yes,' replied the stranger.

They looked at him.

'You're a funny colour,' they said. 'You're not pale, like us.'

'That's because I come from the sunlight,' said the stranger.

They looked at him, baffled. 'Sunlight?'

'Didn't I mention the sunlight?' said the stranger, and his smile spread warmth all around the gloomy village. 'Oh, you must see the sunlight. Some days it is so bright that the tops of the trees sparkle like stars. Some days it breaks through the clouds in pillars of gold. Some days it shines through the rain in a great arc of colours.' He looked at them. 'Don't tell me, you've never seen the sunlight,' he said. They shook their heads. 'Then I will take you there, straightaway,' he declared. 'Follow me and we'll climb to the top!'

As he said this, great debate broke out in the village. I could hear some villagers shouting that the stranger was mad. Others claimed that he was from a rival village, from their enemies; and that he was deliberately luring them into the trees so that he could push them off. But some looked at the colour of his skin and the brightness of his eyes and believed him.

He moved to the edge of the clearing and started to climb. And as he began to climb through the trees again, some followed him. I watched them as they disappeared into the distance above the clearing. Some of them gave up halfway – they found the climb too difficult. But a few followed the stranger right up into the highest branches, until they were lost from sight.

'That's it,' said the village wise men. 'We'll never see them again.'

The villagers went back to their task.

'And so ended the first visit,' continued the computer voice. 'Every now and again, the people from the treetops would come down to the village and tell the others what they had found. They explained how there was enough room for everyone to live up top. Sometimes people from the village returned with them. The rest of the people however, laughed at these tales. And they stayed pale and cold on the forest floor, where their eyes were accustomed to the gloom.'

The voice faded to silence. There was nothing except the distant cries of the jungle animals and birds. The dappled shadows suddenly seemed darker, more menacing.

I looked at Lydia.

'Very nice,' I said. I was whispering, although I didn't know why. 'A bit twee in places. Not very subtle.'

'Oh, well, I'm sure you did your best,' she replied.

'I'm sorry?'

'Well you wrote it,' she replied.

'I didn't!'

'You certainly did.' She spoke to the Ultranet. 'Bibliographic details, please.'

The gentle voice of the storyteller returned. 'The story has been visualised from "Collected Stories of Nick Page". Published posthumously by QuickBuck Conglomerates, 2032. Total sales figures twenty-seven.'

'Twenty-seven?' I exploded. 'Twenty-seven copies!'

'Well,' said Lydia. 'You were slightly passé by then.' She thought for a moment. 'Actually you were passé before you started, but we won't go into that. Anyway, the point of the story —'

'I can't believe it,' I grumbled. 'Twenty-seven copies —'

'Oh stop being so self-obsessed,' snapped Lydia. 'Authors! I ask you. And you have the nerve to accuse me of vanity. Let's get back to the point of the story. Do you want to speak to any of the characters?'

'Er . . . pardon?'

'This is a Virtuality narrative,' explained Lydia very slowly. 'It's based on your story, but the whole point of Virtuality narratives is that you can interact with them. The Ultranet computes their responses.' She looked at me encouragingly. 'Go on,' she said. 'Have a look round the village. Talk to them.'

'Oh. Okay.'

I walked into the village. That is, I *thought* I walked into the village. I knew that, back in the pod my feet weren't moving, but it certainly felt that they were. And, looking down, I could see that they were moving. (Not only that, they were wearing brown, military boots.)

In the centre of the village stood a large, open fire, around which were gathered several villagers. They appeared to be some strange kind of Amazonian/African mixture, like a compact version of the Masai.

'Er ... hello there,' I said.

'Wotcha,' said one of the villagers.

'Oh. You speak English.'

The tribesman looked at me witheringly. 'Since we're fictional characters, we speak whatever you want us to speak.'

'Ah. Yes. Of course. I just wasn't expecting the ... er ... south London accent.'

'It's a random selection. I can change accent if you like.' He thought for a moment. 'I can do Geordie,' he said proudly.

'No, no, it's fine,' I replied. 'So ... how's life?'

'Oh, not bad,' replied the tribesman. 'A bit gloomy, as you can see, but you'll soon get used to that. That's just the way life is, innit?'

'But didn't you listen to what the stranger said?' I asked. 'He talked about sunlight. He offered to take you up there.'

'Oh *that*!' said the tribesman, dismissively. 'If you believe that, you'll believe anything. There is no "up there". There's only more shadow. Just higher up.'

'But why don't you go and find out? All it takes is a bit of climbing. You just have to start.'

'Why should we start climbing? We're happy here. Life's sorted. We go out in the morning and do a spot of hunting. Then we sit down in the evening and stare at the fire for a bit. Then we get drunk on fermented fruit juice.'

'Doesn't seem much of a life.'

'Maybe not, but it's ours!' said the tribesman, fiercely. 'We don't need to have it disturbed by people spreading lies about treetops and sunlight and all that.'

'But aren't you at least intrigued by the idea?' I was getting frustrated. The gloom on the forest floor was making me ache to see the light.

'Nah, not really,' he said. 'Life's sorted, innit? All right, it's a bit dark, I grant you. But we're settled. We know what to expect. We don't need all those sunlighters coming down and disturbing us.'

'Do they come down often?'

'Oh no. Mostly they stay up top, or wherever it is they go. They used to visit quite a lot, I've heard, but nowadays they hardly set foot in the place. We occasionally hear them shouting down at us, and sometimes they send down leaves with bits of writing on them all about the sunlight. But they're not part of our world anymore.'

'Right.' There was a long, rather sad pause. 'Apparently I wrote all this,' I said, at last. 'This is my story.'

'Oh yes?' he said, puffing his pipe. 'In a bad mood were you?'

'I don't know. I don't remember writing it.'

The tribesman nodded.

'Yeah,' he said. 'I have days like that.' He held up a wooden cup. 'Especially when I've been drinking this. Fancy a half of fermented paw-paw juice?'

'No thanks,' I replied. 'I ought to be getting back . . .' I said, standing up. 'Someone's waiting for me.'

'Nice meeting you,' said the tribesman. 'Stay loose. Come back soon. Don't be a stranger!'

I walked back to the edge of the clearing to where Lydia appeared to be having a long and animated conversation with a tapir. He scuttled off when he saw me coming.

'Were you talking to that animal?'

'Not really,' she said. 'He turned out to be an advert for plastic surgery; something to do with nose jobs. I tell you, those adverts get everywhere. Had a good time?'

'Terrific. Let's get back to the light, please.'

When we took the glasses off, the egg-pod was filled once again with the dull afternoon light of London. But at least it was the *real,* dull afternoon light. I looked around me. This was a different jungle. The shadows were lighter. But everywhere the people lived in the same kind of darkness. We sat there in thought for a moment while all around us the streets of the suburbs lay empty.

'Christianity,' Lydia said at last, 'is – or should be – a brighter, truer, higher reality. In both your age and mine, people settled for so much less. They settled for loveless, lonely, gloomy lives, of momentary pleasure and passing satisfaction. They settled for cynicism and defeatism and a kind of unspoken despair.'

'The mass of men lead lives of quiet desperation,' I said. She looked at me. 'Thoreau said that.'

'Yes. I thought it was rather good.'

'So with all these people trapped in their gloomy realities,' I said, 'why didn't Christianity make more of an impact? I mean, if we've got all this sunshine to spread around, you'd have thought it would have been a lot more visible. So what went wrong?'

She paused. 'We never bothered to climb down from the tree-tops,' she said at last. 'We sat and waited for them to come to us.' She looked out of the pod at the grey world. 'You know, so often in the past we've presented Christianity as a set of beliefs, or a load of doctrine, or a mass of theology. In fact, it's so much more simple than that. Christianity is about life. It's about why we're here in the first place and how life should be lived – in all its fullness and wonder and richness. The first responsibility of the church is to live that life. The second responsibility is to share that life with others. But instead of going and seeking them out, instead of going into and living among them, we shut ourselves away in our Christian ghettos. We climbed into the treetops and showered them with leaves.'

I nodded. 'I remember a long time ago talking to a friend of mine, who was a salesman,' I said. 'I asked him what the secret of successful selling was, and he said, "comfort". He said, you don't expect them to come into your comfort zone, you go into theirs. You go where they feel comfortable, even though it might make you feel bad.'

'Yes,' said Lydia. 'It's called "incarnation". And it means climbing down from our lofty perches and going and seeking people out. Because they won't come to us anymore. They have their own worlds to live in, their own "realities" to numb and confuse them.'

I thought back to my own days. I thought of my village with all the people shut up in their homes, living their own, separate, self-contained lives. And I realised how challenging and difficult it would be to reach into their world and show them something different.

'It's nothing new, is it?' asked Lydia. 'When God realised that the world would no longer come to him, he went to the world. He came down, as it were, from the treetops.'

She smiled.

'And the people walking in darkness, saw a great light.'

Dear Miles,

In my last letter I introduced a couple of Greek words. This letter I want to talk about another one: *tekton*.

In Mark 6, people are amazed when they hear Jesus speak and say, 'Isn't this the carpenter?' and the word which is translated 'carpenter' is *tekton*. Actually, *tekton* means really 'someone who builds'. Jesus might have been a carpenter, but he probably also was a stonemason, since most houses at the time were built out of stone. He probably did a bit of everything; he was a general builder, an odd-job man. If you wanted a hole knocked in your wall, you called in the *tekton*. A *tekton* could build you a table, or fix the leak in your roof. This is quite amazing when you think about it: Jesus worked as an odd-job man. Unknowingly people had holes knocked in their walls by God.

Which more or less sums up incarnation. We are called to represent God, to be his odd-job men and women; to get alongside our neighbours and knock down the walls between the people and their creator.

Incarnation lies at the core of Christian faith. It was incarnation which really shocked the opponents of Christianity; the idea that a god, a noble, supernatural being, could come to earth, become a man and die a criminal's death. Gods simply didn't behave in that way. Gods didn't behave in an undignified manner. Gods didn't attend parties with sinners, cook fish for breakfast, tell funny stories, turn over tables in the Temple. Gods are supposed to be aloof, mystical, unfathomable; they're not supposed to work as odd-job men in obscure Palestinian towns.

But that's exactly what happened.

Christians do not worship a stay-at-home God; they do not worship a remote deity who does not deign to get his hands dirty. They worship a God who was prepared to come down and live among those he sought to save.

So why are so many Christians separate from the world around them? Why does so much of church life actually work against incarnation?

If I think back to my own life as an atheist, I spent time with my friends; I went around with them, went to the movies, enjoyed a meal together. We went to the races and to the pub, and then I became a Christian, and every evening was somehow taken up with meetings. Somehow I didn't do the same things that my mates did any more. Of course, things may be different now, but I still feel that there are significant barriers between church and non-church.

Indeed, the very idea of church is a barrier to many people. They don't feel posh enough or intelligent enough or holy enough to cross the doorstep of the imposing church buildings. Too often church does not reach out into its community, and the community never dares to cross the threshold of the church.

Churches have to take incarnation – involvement in the world – seriously. They have to get alongside the people in their community and live lives that show God in action. This means breaking down barriers between church and community. It is church as *tekton*; fixing what is broken, being on hand for emergencies, bringing light into dark houses and dark lives.

Young people, particularly, want an incarnate religion. They do not want something that separates them from the world around them, and I am not at all convinced that, with their increased ecological and environmental concerns, they want the kind of eastern mysticism that argues that the world is just a veil of illusion. One of the wonderful things about Christianity, it seems to me, is that it does not treat the world as an illusion. It treats the world as an enormous opportunity. The world is a chance to know God; and humans have been given a specific role in looking after that world. Christians are not only supposed to be incarnate in the world, they are responsible for the world. They have a stewardship given by God. If the churches were to become more incarnate in the world, then it would demonstrate that they cared about the world, that they were following their maker's example; that they were taking their responsibilities seriously.

Incarnation should be nothing new to Christians; they've been doing it for centuries. But each generation has to rediscover things for themselves. And there is one group of people for whom genuine incarnation is shockingly new: the people around us. If churches were to embody Christianity with no strings attached, then it would be something startlingly new for a society which has consigned the Christian faith to 'something which a few strange people do on Sunday'.

To be fair, there are many churches which are already putting this into action; demonstrating their care for their community by clearing up litter, running social care schemes, cleaning up gardens, supporting the elderly and housebound, and many more innovative schemes. I read somewhere that one church explains this emphasis by saying that their job is to 'love people until they ask why'.

This seems to me something that churches could be exploring. If churches are to be mission churches, they must also be incarnate churches; because how will people hear and understand the good news if the gospel does not live among them?

You know, thinking back to my 'pre-Christian' days makes me sad. Because the truth is, I did enjoy those times.

And much as I value what's happened to me, and what I had with Caroline, I should never have given all that up. I suppose I feel slightly cheated. So much church, so little fun. Sometimes I feel like my life is like the village in Page's fable; a life of shadowy, even gloomy routine. I feel like real life has moved away to the treetops. And I am too old to start climbing trees.

Sorry. I'm sounding depressed. I'm not. Just a little sad. Perhaps I have spent too long living in shadows.

Every good wish,
Stephen

a Visit to the ciRcus

9

As we neared the centre of London, the number of people grew, and the strange, eerie feeling that had persisted in the suburbs ebbed away.

'Where are we going now, then?'

'Dilly-Hub,' said Lydia.

'Sorry?'

'Dilly-Hub,' she repeated. 'Picture Plaza.'

'Um . . . run that past me one more time, will you?'

'I thought you knew London,' she said.

'I do. Or rather, I did. But I don't know what you're talking about. Places change, you know.'

'Yes,' she said. 'Sorry. I forgot. We're going to Dilly-Hub. Can't remember what it used to be called. Has that strange statue in the middle of the guy with the arrow.'

'You mean Piccadilly Circus!'

'That's the one.' She paused. 'Why did you call it circus by the way?'

'I think it came from circle,' I said. 'Just an obsolete term that got stuck, you know how it happens.'

'Yes,' she said. 'I know how it happens.'

We stopped the pod, climbed out and walked into a square filled with people. Piccadilly Circus – Dilly-Hub – had certainly changed. The buildings looked the same, but the lights were something entirely new. The entire space was awash with lights and shapes. It wasn't just the billboards and the advertisements, it was physical light; light moulded into shapes; balloons of ethereal colour floating around filling Piccadilly Circus like huge, multicoloured jellyfish. The lights were no longer the large flat screens of memory, these were huge, pulsating three-dimensional images. Advertising logos floated around or bounced off buildings or danced little jigs. A huge Coca-Cola logo headed straight towards me and then right through me. Across the road I could see a thirty-foot-high Ronald McDonald climbing the side of a building while eating a burger – but this was no solid model but a huge shape of light through which you could see the building behind it. The people in the square walked, almost oblivious, through the pulsating sculptures of light that were coruscating and crackling around them.

'This is amazing!' I murmured. 'It . . . it's beautiful . . .'

Lydia smiled and shrugged. 'I suppose we get used to it.'

'But look at it!' I shouted excitedly, as a massive gin and tonic bounced off the buildings. 'How do they do it? How do they create these shapes?'

'Holographic imaging,' said Lydia, walking casually through a seven-foot-wide pair of luminous M&S underpants. 'Physical light.' She shrugged. 'It's just advertising.'

'It's not like any advertising I've ever seen.'

'No,' she said. 'It wouldn't be, would it? Every age creates its own communication, its own language, music, art. And it's never like anything that has gone before. Wait here. I'm going to get us something to drink.'

As she walked off across Dilly-Hub, I stared open mouthed at the light display. Many of the images were familiar to me – the major multinational corporations that had dominated my time were still very much alive and kicking. But along with Pepsi and Burger King and Sony there were new products. 'EZ-Brite Electro Kleen Aid', 'STS – The Straight-to-Synapse News Service', 'Virtumanity – The Artificial People People'. The colours, the shapes, were completely disorientating.

Suddenly a strange figure appeared in front of me. 'Hello, Citizen!' It said. 'Just a reminder to buy Pixie!' I blinked. I was looking at a three-foot-high elf. It had all the elf stuff – the beard, pointy hat and a little pipe sticking out of his mouth. He inhaled and sighed happily.

'I'm sorry?' I said.

'Pixie Products make the best marijuana you can buy.'

'Are you trying to sell me drugs?' I asked. 'Only I thought people usually saw the pixies after they've been smoking.'

The elf didn't appear to hear me. Instead it disappeared completely. But from another part of the square I could hear the voice, 'Hello, Citizen. Just a reminder to buy Pixie . . .'

I was shocked to see drugs sold so openly, but as I looked around I realised that a whole load of products like it were now freely available and openly advertised. Not just marijuana and recreational drugs but more graphic images, images that, in my time, had been mainly found plastered inside the phone boxes of Piccadilly rather than depicted thirty feet up in full colour. Times certainly had changed. I started to wander around, staring up into the sky. It was like the best light show that you have ever seen. In the distance, I was sure that I could hear the whirring sound of Pink Floyd's lighting designer revolving in his grave.

'Hey Man! Wtch yr stp!'

In my distraction I had walked straight into another man. A big man. Around six foot. Wide. He probably weighed less than a tank, but it would have been a close-run thing.

'Sorry,' I said. 'I'm a stranger here ...'

'Yr gng 2 b sry,' he said. 'F U dnt gt outa my wy.'

I shook my head. His speech was such a rapid flow of words it sounded like someone gargling.

'Nope,' I replied. 'Didn't get that at all. Could you speak a bit slower please?'

It was, apparently, the wrong thing to say. He started to turn pink and wisps of steam started to come out of his nostrils.

'U bazzin me?' he snarled. 'U tkng it, u ltl jfry?'

I shook my head again. 'Nope. You've lost me again. Look, if you're going to insult me, it would be better if you could do it in English. Then I can have a go back.'

He came very close and held up his fist. It was the size of a leg of pork.

'U wnt sm f this?'

'Ah,' I said. ' I understood that. Kind of a universal language there, fat boy.'

The pink turned to crimson.

'Wht U say? Wht U say 2 me?' he stuttered.

'You're a big man,' I said. 'But I'm faster.' And I turned to run. Or I would have if there hadn't been a child standing right behind me. I tried to swerve to avoid the tiny figure, lost my footing and fell to the ground. The child looked down at me. Only it wasn't a child. It wasn't even real.

'Hello Citizen,' it said, 'just a reminder to buy Pixie ...'

I tried to get up to run again, but before I could regain my footing I felt someone grab my collar and lift. Then I was hanging in the air, spinning round as Fat Boy held me six inches off the ground. His eyes were tiny black dots in a huge dough-ball face. They glittered with anger.

'I should warn you that I'm a dead man,' I garbled. 'So technically what you are doing here is desecrating a grave ...'

'Ths tm u going 2 gt it!' he snarled. He held me, helplessly dangling, feet desperately scrabbling for purchase, while his other hand, started to draw back. His fist looked roughly the size of a bunch of bananas. This was going to hurt.

'You wouldn't hit an old woman with a wooden leg would you?' I said, desperately.

The arm reached its trigger point, and I shut my eyes waiting for the blow.

Instead, I was dropped to the ground. Cautiously I opened my eyes and looked up. There was a strange expression on the man's face. He appeared to have gone cross-eyed, and his face was purple. His tiny, black eyes were screwed up in agony and the steam that had been coming from his nose was now coming out of his ears. A long, slow hiss escaped from his lips and he started to collapse. It was like watching a hot-air balloon deflating. As I scrambled back to my feet, he went in the other direction, sinking to the ground to reveal, behind him, the slight, white-haired form of Lydia. Disconcertingly, she was holding two plastic cups.

'Now,' she said kindly, looking down at him. 'I'm very sorry to have had to kick you. But you see, my friend here, as well as being hugely irritating, is a stranger. So he simply doesn't understand our ways.'

Fat Boy didn't reply. Or rather, he did, but all he managed to say was 'Urrrrggghhyhghghhgh.'

She reached down and patted him on the head. And suddenly her voice changed. 'Don't worry,' she said. 'I'm sure they'll grow back.' She moved to go, then remembered something and turned back to the figure on the floor. 'And F U cm nr us agn,' she gargled, 'U cn hv sm mor F it.' She turned to me sweetly. 'Shall we go?' she said.

We walked away from the lights and started to make our way down what I recognised as Haymarket. Lydia, rather grumpily, thrust a cup at me.

'Honestly,' she said. 'I can't leave you alone for a minute, can I? What did you have to go and get into a fight for?'

'I didn't start it,' I protested. 'I couldn't understand him. And then I tried to run and fell over a nonexistent pixie.' I looked at her in admiration. 'Anyway, how does an old lady get the strength to kick like that?'

'It's not about, strength,' she said. 'It's about strategic placement. It's not about how hard, it's about where.'

'Where did you kick him, then?'

'Right in the middle of Dilly-Hub.'

'Painful.'

'Anyway, we'd better not hang around. I don't suppose he's over-endowed with brain cells, but it would be better not to hang around and find out.'

'I didn't mean to get into a fight,' I explained. 'I just bumped into him, and then he started talking, and I couldn't understand what he was saying. It was all garbled.'

'He was speaking txt,' she said.

'Sorry?'

'Txt,' she repeated. 'It's a kind of dialect. Like English with the vowels taken out. It all started on mobile phones in your time. People started writing it and now they talk it.'

'You mean they turned text messaging into a dialect?'

'Why not? It's only another way of communicating, after all.'

'Well I didn't understand a word of it.'

'No,' she said. 'It's a language. And you have to learn it.'

We walked on through the streets that, at the same time, looked hauntingly familiar, and startlingly different, until we emerged into a well-known London landmark.

'Trafalgar Square!' I exclaimed. 'This hasn't changed at all! It's nice to know that some things have remained the same.'

'Er ... well, not quite,' said Lydia. 'We renamed it. It's called Picture Plaza now. You know, because of all the galleries all around.'

I looked up at Nelson.

'So much for the Battle of Trafalgar,' I said. 'You lost out to the National Gallery.'

'Well, it wasn't really our choice,' said Lydia. 'We had to rename it after the EU Pacification Ruling.'

'The what?'

'All places named after battles were deemed to be incitements to violence and racial conflict,' she said. 'Trafalgar Square was lucky. You can't imagine what they renamed Waterloo.'

I imagined.

'So we called it Picture Plaza. Because of all the galleries,' continued Lydia. 'The National Gallery and the National Portrait Gallery were there in your time, of course. But now we've added to them. We've got the National Gallery of Graphic Design over there, the National Postcard Gallery in that corner and over there –' she pointed at a church building, 'the National Gallery of Graffiti.'

'Graffiti? People go and look at graffiti?'

'Of course,' she said. 'We recognise it as a unique late-twentieth-century art form.' She smiled. 'You should have seen the visiting exhibition from the Guggenheim last year. "Killroy

Was 'Ere" it was called. A collection of walls and public lavatories from around the world. Ah yes, there were some geniuses with spray cans in your day.'

I looked at the gallery, which was now advertising an exhibition entitled 'Roy Luvs Sharon – Romantic Graffiti of the Late 1970s'.

'That used to be a church,' I said. 'St Martin's-in-the-Fields.'

'Yes,' she said. 'But places change. Be thankful it didn't turn into a hotel like the rest of them in London.'

'And now it's just a home for graffiti.'

'Yes, but we don't think of it in that way anymore. We don't think of graffiti as vandalism. Different cultures do this all the time. Things that were once discarded become collectable. Artistic expressions that were once dismissed as trivial or "low-art" become valued and celebrated. And languages change. And if you don't learn how to speak to the people around you, you end up getting badly beaten.'

'I can hear the heavy footsteps of another lesson,' I sighed. 'But believe me, it's nothing I've not heard before.'

'Outside the churches in your time, language was constantly changing. But inside, it was like some kind of freezer, where language was preserved against the ravages of time.' She laughed. 'I mean what were you thinking of?' she asked. 'All that ridiculous anachronistic, arcane language you lot spouted every Sunday. Did none of you ever think about how it sounded to the outsider? Did no-one ever consider that there might be people sitting in their church who simply hadn't got a clue what anyone was talking about?'

'I've said all this,' I sighed. 'I said it till I was blue in the face. But it's hard for people to change their jargon. It's part of what defines them as a culture. It's part of what makes them distinctive.'

'Yes, but like I said right at the beginning of this journey,' continued Lydia, 'there's a difference between being distinctive and being incomprehensible. You grew up in the church. I came in from the outside. I remember being entirely bewildered. All those images which once meant something but which had become completely obscure. All those theological words that we never bothered to explain because we thought that people still knew our language. All those songs we sung . . .'

'I know what you mean,' I said. 'I mean, I liked the hymns, but some of the language was rather difficult . . .'

'I wasn't talking about hymns,' she snapped. 'At least when the hymn writers wrote they were using the language of the people around them. "Redemption" meant something in the seventeenth century because people were still being kidnapped into slavery and had to be bought back. So they were using contemporary terms. The writers of your time hardly made that effort.'

'What do you mean?'

'I remember sitting in your church once and looking through the song book,' she said. 'In all the songs, I couldn't find one twentieth-century image. Not one. I mean, there we were in the era of the jet plane and the spaceship and we were still singing about two-edged swords and bunches of grapes and sheep.'

'Biblical images,' I protested.

'Just because they're in the Bible doesn't make them sacred. Jesus used those pictures because people knew what they meant. People could look up and see vineyards and sheep and soldiers with swords. They were images to convey holy truth. It was the truth that we should have been concentrating on. It was that we should have been preserving. Instead we canonised the images, we preserved the old pictures at all costs. These old, outdated, unhelpful images became holy in themselves, so that you couldn't have a worship song unless it was filled with sheep and swords and banners and people being "refined by fire".' She laughed. 'I mean, what was it with all that refining fire bit? How many people do you think understood that image? Did I miss something? Was the early twenty-first-century church filled to the brim with an in-depth knowledge of smelting? Or was it, as I rather suspect, just that most worship songwriters couldn't be bothered to find a better image?'

'I think they were just rather committed to the Bible,' I said. 'So they tended to use the biblical images whenever they could.'

'That's all very well. I wish everyone in your churches had been committed to the Bible. But just because you're committed to the Bible doesn't mean you have to swallow its language lock, stock and water jar. Just because you want to tell people the message of the Bible doesn't mean that you have to speak in Aramaic.'

'So what should we have done?'

'What we really needed were new metaphors,' she said. 'New images that would convey God's love. And new words to convey the truth in. I mean people would walk into churches and not understand a single thing from beginning to end. And I don't just mean the traditional services, I mean all of them.'

'So are you suggesting that we should change the language we use?'

'If it doesn't alter the meaning, yes. Words change over time, don't they? Circus might have meant "circle" to the people who named Piccadilly, but in our time it meant a large tent with very, very unfunny clowns. We should have kept checking that the words were working. Instead we were sloppy and lazy. It was far easier to fill our songs and our sermons with antiquated images that meant nothing. Thinking up new metaphors is hard work.'

'But surely there are some images that are eternal?'

'I suppose so,' she said. 'But even then you've got to keep reminding people. After all what did a cross symbolise to people of your time? Didn't it symbolise Christianity rather than Christ? Didn't it symbolise a slightly soft, slightly archaic folk-religion? When really, the cross was two pieces of wood where they nailed God. Two pieces of wood where God proved how much he loved us. That's the truth that should never be forgotten.' She pointed to the top of the Gallery of Graffiti, where atop the former church, the timeless image still stood.

'An image is only effective if we can see the reality it points to. Language is only effective if people can understand truth through it. When it mystifies them, when the words obscure the meaning instead of reveal it, it's time to find different words. When you get back, tell your people to keep talking about the cross – but make sure people understand the meaning.

'That's the thing about language,' she said. 'Get it right and the symbols are incredibly powerful.' She smiled. 'It's not strength. It's strategic placement.'

Dear Miles,

After reading this chapter I did think of writing something on emerging technologies and their impact on the church. But I fear I am too old a dog to investigate these new tricks. And anyway emerging technologies are just means to an end. What Page is talking about here is language.

As you know, the New Testament was written in what is known as Koine Greek. *Koine* means 'common'. It wasn't the smooth, stylish Greek of the philosophers. It wasn't written in Latin, the political language of empire, and it wasn't written in the 'theological' language of Hebrew. It wasn't even written in Aramaic – the language Jesus would have spoken.

This was always a bit of a problem for many Christian scholars. Koine is a relatively recent discovery. For a long time scholars struggled with the Greek of the New Testament because it simply wasn't posh enough. They called it 'degenerate Attic' because compared with the Greek of the great Athenian writers and philosophers, it wasn't very good. It was not until the discovery of a wide range of ordinary letters and trade documents that they realised that the New Testament authors had deliberately chosen to speak in the language of the ordinary man. The Greek seemed common because it *was* common; it was *Koine*. It was the language of the ordinary, average trader or workman, the type of language that was found throughout much of the Mediterranean area at that time.

Now the most obvious reason for the New Testament writers using Koine Greek was one of mass communication. Koine Greek was spoken throughout the ancient Mediterranean world. It was spoken on the streets of Lyon, Rome, Alexandria, and Jerusalem. Even the Emperor Marcus Aurelius kept his diary in Greek. So by using Koine the writers opened Christianity up to all people; not just an educated elite or a chosen nation.

More than that, however, it also made the point that Christianity was a religion that was not afraid of the ordinary. The great doctrines and tenets of Christianity were not fashioned in fancy phrases but in the ordinary words of ordinary people.

And the issue still hasn't gone away. Throughout history there have been repeated attempts to speak about Christianity in the common language. Luther challenged the use of Latin and translated the New Testament into German. Wycliffe died because he translated it into English. Every so often someone emerges who tells the tale anew in the language of their people. And generally speaking, all their hard work is undone by theologians and preachers and hymn writers.

I believe the church today desperately needs to rediscover what it means to speak in the common language. Part of the reason why non-Christians don't respond to the gospel message is that they simply don't understand it. We're using terms that mean nothing to them. The common language has moved on, but the church is still using language and images from bygone eras.

The argument is, of course, that these are biblical terms, but the question is whether they are relevant and meaningful in a mission context. That doesn't mean rejecting all the terms that we use in Christianity. Words like *salvation*, *incarnation*, *redemption* have rich and powerful meanings. But only if you explain them. If you just throw them out, all you will do is mystify your audience. And that includes many people sitting in the pews, silently thinking to themselves 'I've never understood that word.'

Rediscovering a Koine Christianity means not saying 'fellowship' when we simply mean 'friendship'; it means searching for a modern image rather than automatically reaching for one from the Bible; it means using the stories, language and images from the culture around you to communicate the gospel.

I wonder also, if the attempt to speak in a relevant manner might also broaden itself beyond language. Costume, for example, is a language; perhaps we ought to ask ourselves what messages the vestments and clerical garb give out.

The vestments used by the church owe their origin not to some idea of what the Hebrew priests used but to the common, secular costume of the world in which the early church grew up. The development of a specifically 'priestly' garb dates from somewhere between the fourth and ninth centuries; it's not something that dates back to the origins of Christianity.

Some clerical garb is an even later invention. The dog-collar, which we all associate with vicars, ministers and priests, is an invention of the late nineteenth century. Some claim it was invented by a priest called Rosiminian Luigi Gentili so that Roman Catholic priests in England, forbidden by the civil law to wear their cassocks in public, could be recognised by their flocks. According to the *Glasgow Herald* of 6 December 1894, it was invented by the Rev. Dr Donald McLeod. Whatever the case, it only gained general acceptance just before the first world war. It's seen as traditional, but it really isn't. And more to the point, what message does it send out? That vicars can't do their own ties? That there is something holy about wearing half a washing up liquid bottle around your neck?

Sometimes, in the right setting, clerical vestments inspire respect and even awe. Most of the time, however, I feel they just provoke bewilderment. I recall speaking to an old student of mine who was a television producer. He was talking to me about the many complaints he got from

Christians that he wouldn't allow them to air their views on his programme. 'I do allow them,' he told me. 'But they look weird and no-one can understand a word they say.'

We have an uncommon God. Which makes it all the more important that we talk about him in a common language. That's what Paul did. That's what Luke and James and John and all the writers of the New Testament did.

And I don't suppose they were wearing a dog collar at the time, either.

Ever yours,
Stephen

ReAl Life

From Picture Plaza, we walked south, down Whitehall. The road was empty of traffic and I noticed it had been entirely paved with a soft, green substance that made me feel as though I was walking on rubber. As we progressed, the thoroughfare became increasingly crowded with statues. At the north end there were only one or two, but then they began to proliferate; they were stuffed into doorways, crammed into niches, high on walls, or mounted in the middle of the pavement on huge, stone slabs. Whitehall had always had its fair share of monuments, but now they appeared to have been breeding.

'Is it me,' I asked Lydia, 'or are there more statues here than there were before?'

'Yes, they gathered them all together here when they closed down the parks,' explained Lydia.

'They closed down the parks?'

'Of course,' she said. 'Every city did. All that prime building land just going to waste. We don't have parks now. We have machines to give us exercise and air-conditioning to give us fresh air.'

I looked around me. Military leaders jostled with politicians. There was Wellington on a horse, and next to him Winston Churchill. A marble statue of a young Queen Victoria nestled next to a rather tatty looking bronze of Lord Byron. There was a figure of King Charles II, holding a scroll and looking for all the world as though he couldn't wait to get back to the horseraces. Next to him was a more modern statue, to judge by its appearance. It was mounted on a horse, holding a large book and looked vaguely familiar. I looked at the inscription.

'Dale Winton?' I asked. 'Dale Winton? And what's he doing on a horse?'

Lydia looked almost reverential.

'Every city has its tribute to Lord Winton,' she said. 'He was the first British President of United Europe. One of the greatest leaders we ever had.'

'Are we talking about the same Dale, here?' I asked. 'The supermarket sweep Dale?'

'That's the one.'

'And he became President of Europe?'

'Yes,' she said. 'It was a printing error, really, but by the time they'd found out he'd already been sworn in. And he proved a marvellous success.' She looked up. 'Alright, maybe the horse is a bit over the top, but they've caught the tan wonderfully.'

We walked on, through this jungle of stone and bronze, this increasingly labyrinthine street full of famous faces and forgotten heroes. For, while some of the statues were familiar, many more of them were obscure figures; ancient heroes cryogenically sealed in marble or dull, oxydised metal, their reputations ignored, their names no longer recalled, the wars in which they had gained their reputations now consigned to the dustbin of history.

'Do people come here much?' I asked Lydia.

'Oh yes,' she said. 'It's a great place to sleep.'

'Sorry?'

'For a start it's always dry.'

She pointed upwards. I looked up and, through the gathering gloom, I could see that there was a thin, almost transparent membrane stretched over the road, as if someone had stretched a huge sheet of cling-film between the buildings.

'They put up the cover to protect the statues from the worst of the acid-rain,' she said. 'And, because a lot of these statues were designated as great art, they installed street-heaters and humidity controls. All of which means that this street is a great place to kip down for the night, if you're homeless. It's warm and it's dry. So at night, this place is a community all of its own.'

Now that I looked, I could see signs of what she meant. Under one huge bronze horse, someone had lain out their sleeping mat. Behind and between several of the statues, tarpaulins and plastic sheets had been arranged into shelters. Someone had even hung their socks to dry on a sword carried by William Pitt the Younger.

'You've got to laugh, really,' said Lydia. 'The authorities fondly believed that if they gathered all these ancient statues together in one place, then people would come for the culture,' Lydia explained. 'They believed that they were providing a palace of culture, a massive collection of fine art. But actually what they were providing was a hotel room.'

We sat down on one of the plinths. Behind us, another bronze statue of some forgotten First World War general stared out into the late afternoon light, as hard and unyielding as he had been on the day he ordered all those men to their deaths.

'It was the same with the parks,' Lydia explained. 'They thought they knew why people went there. According to all the research, people went there for exercise, or to play on the swings, or to walk their dogs. So, they reasoned, as long as we provide them with alternatives for those activities, we'll be all right. They thought that if they replaced the parks with gyms and biomechanical exercise centres and virtual recreation spaces then no-one would miss them. What they didn't realise is that part of the reason why people go to parks is because they are parks. Because, as well as the activities, they liked the atmosphere. The people wanted to feel the grass under their feet. They wanted to see the greenery, to smell the flowers, to be outside. They went to the spaces because they were spacious.'

She waved her arm about. 'And all these . . .' she continued. 'Oh, some people come to study the art, some people come because they like the history. But every night, thousands come because they want somewhere warm and dry. The important thing is to find out why people come and what they really want.' She smiled.

'It's the same with churches.'

'Do you know,' I said, 'I thought it might be.'

She ignored the sarcasm. 'In our churches,' she said, 'we rarely stopped to ask what people were actually needing. We assumed that they were all coming for the same thing; that they were coming to worship God or talk about theology. But many people in our churches were coming because they were lonely or because they were scared or because they were unsure. And we never talked about those issues enough. People came to church for any number of reasons – and not always the reasons we assume. They brought with them all manner of burdens, and it was up to us, as representatives of Christ, to give them rest. Except we didn't do that. We just assumed we knew why they were there and then carried on in our old, familiar way. So they came with their questions, their burdens, their worries, and they found . . . what? Answers to questions they never asked; solutions for problems they didn't have. Words they simply weren't interested in.'

'You're talking about the language again . . .'

'No, I'm talking about the content. How we speak to people – that's the first thing. We use their language, their symbols. But *what* we say to them is even more vital. The church of your day spent so much time talking about things that simply didn't matter. Synods spent years debating one word of liturgy. Preachers talked for hours on subjects that had no possible relevance to anyone in their congregation. Shelves of books were written on theories and subjects that had no discernible link to real life.'

I smiled. 'I remember going into my local Christian bookstore once and looking for the "Contemporary Issues" section,' I said. 'When I eventually found it, it consisted of seven books on the bottom shelf at the back of the shop. And three of those books were about angels.'

'Exactly. And even when they did concentrate on contemporary life, they managed to find the less important parts. It's the Harry Potter syndrome.'

'Sorry?'

'You remember Harry Potter? Big publishing phenomenon. I remember when the books came out. There we had a world full of war and terror, a world where millions were dying of malnutrition, where children were being born into slavery, where drugs were rampant and violence was endemic. A world where people flew planes into buildings, and greed and avarice wiped out whole communities around the world. And the burning issue for Christians was "should I let my child read Harry Potter?"'

'Well it was kind of important –'

'Not compared to the other stuff!' she snapped. 'Not compared to the real issues.' She threw up her arms in exasperation. 'No non-Christians were worried about that. They were worried about how they could keep their marriage together, about how they could cope with their children, how to keep their jobs. They had *real* problems. We had ethical issues derived from children's books.' She paused. 'Have you ever wondered how many sermons you will hear in your life? Let's say you hear 50 sermons a year. And you go to church from the time you are eighteen to the time you are seventy. That's 2600 sermons. And how many will you actually remember?' She thought for a moment. 'I think I can remember four sermons.' She paused. 'And none of them were yours.'

'Thanks. You're always so encouraging.'

She ignored me. 'The point is *why* don't we remember them? Because so often they don't connect with reality. They either say the same things over and over again, or they talk about things that simply don't matter to the people listening. Every week, in your time, people will come into your churches and go away again, without making any link with real life. Sunday morning is never linked with Monday to Friday.'

'Okay. I'll buy that. So how do we find out? How do we find out what people need to know?'

'We ask them of course. We engage with the congregation and ask them what they need to know about. We try to find out why they go to church and what they need from us.'

'But you can't address everyone's needs, every week.'

'Of course not. And there has to be room for God to work, for an inspired, unexpected message to strike home. But the key thing is application. I was always struck by Paul's letters. All we ever heard about in the churches I used to go to was his theology – or versions of it at any rate. We rarely heard about the way he ended every letter with application.' She smiled. 'Every time he wrote to a church he ended up with suggestions as to what they could actually *do* in their lives to change things. He understood, you see, that Christianity wasn't just some airy-fairy theories. It wasn't just something that you discussed or argued about or explored on a theoretical level. It was something that should take over and change our lives.'

She paused for a moment. In the dim afternoon light, she suddenly seemed to glow with energy and passion, and I caught a vision of the girl she had once been, the woman she would one day, before God, be again.

'When God came to earth,' she said, 'he came as a human, not as an idea. Paul knew that. He knew that Christ came to offer real help to real people in need. He came to lift people's burdens from their shoulders, to change the way they behaved, to change their attitudes to their work, their homes and their families. Those are the things that people care about. Those are where we should have centred our teaching. We should have made it real for people. Because it is real. Jesus Christ isn't some statue to be polished and admired; he's a person to be encountered. God cares about reality. Otherwise he wouldn't have made it.'

'So what should we do?'

'Find out why people are in church. Find out what they want to hear about. Ask people in your community or district what they want help with. Make sure you know what people really need, before you try to provide it for them.'

I looked around, aware of a growing sense of movement, of a rustling, shuffling noise, of a shift in the air. As the late afternoon light began to dim, people were converging on the area around the statues, like birds coming home to roost. They were shuffling, bulky figures, weighed down with bags, stratified with layer upon layer of ragged clothing. They were returning home from wherever their expedition had led them, bearing with them treasures retrieved from the city's refuse, and the pathetic detritus of their own lives. Slowly, they began to settle down in their places, like animals returning to their burrows. There, beneath the famous and the feted, lived the unloved and the unwanted.

I thought back to the parades and processions which had once made their way down Whitehall, in all their pomp and ceremony. Here was a ceremony of a different sort. Here was a procession of the lonely, the trooping of the dispossessed; their uniform no more than dirty rags; their regiments gathering together because sharing loneliness is always better than being alone. They were the waste products of the consumer culture, unwanted, unacknowledged, unloved; they were the people society threw away.

'Nothing changes, really,' I said. 'They look exactly like the people I saw on the streets all those years ago.'

'The poor are always with us,' said Lydia. 'And they always look the same. They always look like Jesus.'

Soon, the spaces between the statues became more crowded. The atmosphere became noisier. People began to light fires, to arrange their belongings around them, to lay out their mats. Old arguments were brought out and dusted down, familiar friendships were resumed. While I sat there watching, an entire community had somehow sprung into life in between the statues and the plinths and the tributes to former glories.

Lydia lapsed into silence. Minutes ticked by slowly and gradually our presence began to attract more attention. More than one person stared at us with suspicion. Darkness began to fall and I started to feel slightly nervous.

'Lydia,' I whispered, 'shouldn't we be going? What are we waiting for?'

She turned to me and smiled.

'We're waiting to meet someone,' she replied.

'Here?'

'Of course.'

I looked around. I couldn't see anyone who would give us any help on our quest. I could see several people who would probably give us a swig of something alcoholic and several who could pass on some unusual skin infections, but no-one you might call 'informative'.

And then, I heard a voice.

Coming through the crowded street was a young girl in a duffel-coat. Well, I say duffel-coat; the thing was so old and shapeless and battered that it was difficult to guess what it had once been. For all I could see it could have started out life as an anorak. Or a greatcoat. Or possibly an offcut piece of carpet. Her hair was a kind of very light ginger; that shade that cannot decide whether to be a blonde or a redhead. It was swept back from her forehead by her Putershades, which she was wearing as a kind of Alice band. On her feet were a huge pair of black boots. She looked clownish; like a child dressed in a grown-up's clothes.

As she made her way towards us, she stopped to talk to the people in the shelters. Some of them greeted her with warmth and friendliness. Some of them were suspicious and surly. Quite a few issued nothing more than a stream of swearwords. It didn't seem, however, to phase her. She carried on, moving from shelter to shelter, from person to person. And the reason I picked her out above the crowd was the laughter. The laughter I had previously heard in this bleak place was harsh and threatening; laughter at someone's pain or misfortune. But this laughter lifted you and cheered you. The girl's laughter brought something rare into this dark place: it brought joy. It was a butterfly-joy; fragile, fluttering, transient. But beautiful.

The girl gradually made her way towards us. Then she spotted Lydia and waved enthusiastically. She stopped and, putting her head on one side, looked at me. Then she smiled. Lydia beckoned her over.

She was young and pretty and bubbling with life. Over her shoulder she carried an old canvas bag, which appeared to be crammed with old bits of paper.

'Lydia!' she exclaimed, giving her a kiss. 'I'm so glad you could make it.'

'I said I'd be here, didn't I?' said Lydia, with her typical abruptness, but the girl just laughed.

'Yes you did.' She turned to me. 'And you brought him with you.'

'Of course.'

Lydia turned to me.

'Nick,' she said, 'this is Petra.'

I held out a hand.

'Nice to meet you,' I said. Her hand was tiny. In fact, she was tiny.

'Hi, Granddad,' said Petra. 'You know, for a dead man you're looking really well.'

I froze. All of a sudden the world started to spin.

'What did you ... How ... Who?' I spluttered.

'This is your granddaughter,' said Lydia. 'I thought it would be nice for you two to meet.'

Dear Miles,

Last time I wrote to you about language. However, it's all very well to speak in words that people understand, the next hurdle is to make sure that what you have to say is worth listening to.

One of the commonest criticisms of the church is that somehow it is divorced from real life. Christianity is perceived as being remote from reality, as not being concerned with the everyday lives of ordinary people.

And the sad truth is that many of the people who are making this accusation – even if it is in the quiet of their own hearts – are Christians. Too many Christians sit in their churches on Sunday waiting desperately to hear something that is going to help them on Monday. Too often they hear bland phrases, polished theology, but nothing that is of any use in today's society. It's not that Christianity hasn't got anything to say about real life; it's just that no-one's actually saying it.

You see, the man in the pew is not thinking about the Johannine theory of substitutionary atonement; he's wondering how to keep his marriage together, or how to hold on to his job, or how to stop himself from shouting at his kids. The woman sitting next to him is not thinking about the role of baptism in the early church, but of how she is going to juggle all the jobs she has to do without losing her sanity. But church doesn't say anything about that. Instead it spouts endless doctrine and dogma, it chunters on with its theological terms, it takes refuge in a fairy-land of systematic theology where all the loose ends of life are tidied up and all the nasty stuff that goes on outside the church walls is ignored in the hope that it will go away.

Here, as you are aware, I am touching on a painful topic. I've been trying to keep my own history out of these letters – although I'm sure that when you asked me to read this manuscript, part of your reason was precisely that I should confront my own past. So I'd better begin by stating that I'm not bitter about what happened, and I'm not unaware of my own role in my departure from the church. I'm not trying to blame anyone, it's just that after she went, everything seemed to just fall apart.

I ought to say that the problems I had with the church were not what you might call the emotional ones. When it came to the suffering and the grief, the church was an enormous help. They understood my grief entirely – and, indeed, many of Caroline's friends shared it. They were there with words and actions of comfort and love. No, they could cope with my pain and loneliness and loss. What they found more difficult to cope with was my doubts. Suddenly I was bringing questions, anxieties, bewildering problems that they simply didn't want to confront.

I can't blame them, in a way. Because I hadn't confronted them either. The sad – I might say shameful – fact was that none of my doubts were new. I had lived with these questions about my faith for a long time. I suppose that was part of the problem. That was the shock. It was not that I was shocked to encounter these questions; what was shocking was how long they had lain at the back of my mind, gnawing away. It was the shock of the old. When Caroline died, these questions suddenly burst forward, and along with them the knowledge that for years they had been there, and I had never found the courage to address them.

I was suddenly aware that I had spent many years in church thinking about these issues, while they had hardly ever been addressed from the pulpit or the lectern. I had been carrying these burdens for decades. I felt as though I had spent forty years keeping quiet.

And so I began to leave. I know that you and Susan thought that I left because of Caroline's death; but that is not so. Of course, if C had still been alive I would probably have remained within the bosom of the church, because love lightens all our burdens and stills all our questions. But when she went . . . well, I just lost patience with the church. I was no longer willing to waste my time sitting in the pew in the hopes that I would hear something relevant; I was no longer willing to put up with what seemed like such an imposition on my life. Jesus offers rest for all those who carry heavy burdens. I had a burden and the church showed me nowhere that I could lay it down.

I suppose I was angry at what the church had become. Here was I, a man who had spent a lot of my life studying those first, fiery years of Christianity, stuck in a church which, if faced with a fiery faith, would instinctively reach for the fire extinguisher.

And it's not as if I didn't try to raise these issues. I spoke to lots of people in the church about my concerns, but the shutters seemed to come down. I talked to Donald, our vicar, but it was clear he had me labelled as 'upset old man'. With only a few years to go to his pension and his house in Norfolk, he was hardly likely to embark on a wholesale revamp of the church services.

And so I started to leave.

You know one of the things that is missing from Page's story – one of the many things missing – is *how* people leave church. I suppose because he has been pitched into the far future, into a church where people have already left, he simply can't cover it. But it is an important topic. Because all the research shows that, on the whole, people do not leave churches suddenly. We don't switch from 'churchgoer', to 'non-churchgoer'; instead we quietly drift away. We leave in increments. It starts with one missed week, then two, then we go to church once a month, then once every few months, then at Christmas. Then we don't go at all.

And the thing is that all the people around you hardly notice it happening. Indeed, the more successful the church is, the less they notice people go. If a church of twenty people loses a member that is noticeable; in a church of two hundred it is much easier to slip out of the door without attracting any attention.

I want to emphasise something. I have left the church; I have not abandoned the faith. Perhaps one of the few rays of hope in church decline is that, as far as we can tell, only a minority of church leavers lose their faith entirely. Most church leavers retain their faith; or a version of it. Losing your faith and losing faith in the church are not the same things at all.

Also, it's tempting to think that most of the people who leave churches are fringe people. This too is not necessarily the case. Many leavers had been in positions of responsibility, some had even been part of the leadership.

What happens is that you suddenly realise that your faith journey is taking you in a different direction. With a shock, I woke one Sunday morning and realised that I just didn't need the church any more.

I wonder if church leaders really understand why people have left their churches? Do they take it as a personal affront? Do they put it down to doctrinal failings or backsliding? Most of the leavers I have spoken to felt that they were simply not being listened to. So they stopped trying to be heard.

We often talk about how churches should be visitor-aware; of how they should welcome people and make them feel that they belong. Perhaps churches should also be leaver-aware. Perhaps as well as having a 'Just Looking' group for new Christians, they should have a 'Just Taking Another Look' group for those who have been around a long time. Or a 'Rethinking' group, for those whose original position has shifted somewhat. Or a 'Just Doubting' group. Or, at the opposite end to the 'Alpha' course, we could have an 'Omega' course for those of us who are about to leave the church. Or . . . anything. Anything that helps us deal with these voices. But no. The church, you see, is very good at dealing with the faith of its members. What it can't cope with is the doubts.

It took me some time to finally make the break. And what I have found is that I don't miss the paraphernalia of church. I don't really miss the services, the meetings, the busy-ness. I do miss some of the people, but I still see them frequently. Curiously, hardly any of them talk to me about why I left. Is this just British reserve? Or is it that they really don't want to hear the answers?

This letter has turned out very different to what I expected. Have we ever really spoken of these things? I can't recall. If not, I am very sorry. You are one of my oldest friends. You deserved an explanation.

Will I ever go back? I don't know. Maybe God will send another message to shock me back towards the church. But somehow I think I am past shocking. I suspect that, from here on in, I must voyage alone.

Ever yours,
Stephen

a Visit to cHuRch

There are times in life
when you just have to go along with things, when you just have
to put your reservations behind you and 'move'. Bungee jump-
ing. Escaping from an avalanche. Following a granddaughter you
never knew you had, down a dark passage in a London of the
future, where you've been catapulted due to a bizarre time-
travelling incident. That sort of thing.

The alleyway was dark and smelt of urine. It led away from
Whitehall and wound down between what, I guessed, had once
been government buildings but which were now run-down ten-
ements. Ahead I could make out the silver glow of Lydia's hi-tech
coat and, beyond that, the dim figure of Petra – the girl who was,
much to my surprise, my granddaughter.

'Where are we going?' I whispered to Lydia as we rounded
yet another murky corner.

'We're going to church of course,' she said.

'Church? I thought it was dead.'

'Oh, I never said it was dead,' said Lydia. 'I just said it was
invisible.'

Eventually we came to a tiny, square courtyard, surrounded by old red brick walls. Above us, all around, the walls of the buildings went up, many stories high. Looking at the pipes and grilles that still hung to the sides of the walls, I guessed that at one time this courtyard had been little more than a ventilation shaft in the middle of the main block, a ventilation area that had since been opened up by renovation and renewal, or by the need for more space, which saw the builders burrow further into that dark palace. In the wall to our left, there was a large, rectangular, slab of metal, devoid of any decoration or handle, except for a tiny metal grille at one edge. Petra walked up to it and spoke into the grille.

'Hi, it's me,' she said.

With a rusty, grating noise, the metal slab slid to one side.

'Wow,' I said. 'That is one minimalist front door.'

Petra turned to me and smiled brightly. 'I like it,' she said. 'It always reminds me of the stone rolling away from the tomb. You know, big, heavy ...'

'And situated in an old ventilation shaft,' I said. 'Funny, I don't recall that detail in the New Testament.'

She laughed, and the notes echoed up around the old brickwork. 'You're just like your writing,' she said.

The hallway into which we entered could not have been more of a contrast to the courtyard outside. It was warm and brightly lit and filled with the enticing smell of baking bread. On the walls were pictures; bright splashes of vermilion and crimson and gold which burst into the dimness of the world like fireworks.

I stood there, enjoying the warmth, breathing in the aroma.

'Don't tell me,' I said. 'This is some kind of automatic air-freshener that simulates bread. And the bread machine is called Jimmy and likes nothing better than having a long chat with you.'

'No,' said Petra. 'This is real. But you are clever. The bread machine is called Jimmy, and he's making a fresh batch. And I'm sure he'd love to have a long chat with you.' She walked up to me and looked into my eyes and put a hand, ever so softly, on my cheek. 'Don't be so cynical, Granddad,' she said. 'It doesn't suit you.'

'Please,' I said. 'Don't call me Granddad.'

'But it's true.'

'It's true for you,' I said. 'But where I come from I haven't got any grandchildren and I'm only thirty-nine.'

Lydia looked at me sharply.

'I'm only forty-two,' I corrected. 'And my daughters are all under eight.'

'Daughters!' Petra exclaimed. She looked at Lydia. 'You mean Dad hasn't been born yet?'

There was a long pause.

'Dad?' I said. 'Born?'

'Your son,' explained Petra. 'My father.'

'Don't be ridiculous!' I snapped. 'I haven't got a son.'

'No, well, he was born rather late in life,' said Petra. 'And he did come as a bit of a surprise.'

'But you don't understand!' I said. 'I can't have a son! There are . . . um . . . reasons. He wouldn't be a surprise, he'd be a medical miracle.'

Petra laughed, and for a moment, I caught a glimpse of her grandmother. 'Strange things happen, Granddad,' she said. 'And anyway, look on the bright side: you're about to make a lot of money suing the vasectomy clinic.' And she turned and pushed open a door to reveal a room full of people.

→•←

The room was large and simply furnished. About ten or twelve people were inside, some sitting quietly, some chatting. At one end was a table which a young man was covering with a cloth, and on which he placed a large, wooden cross. It was a crude object, simply made out of two pieces of rough wood which had obviously been retrieved from a skip, but its very clumsiness had a kind of honesty about it, a recognition that the original to which it pointed was not a nice piece of joinery, but a crude tool of execution.

The floor was covered with soft cushions and old woollen rugs and mats. I looked around, but I couldn't see any sign of chairs which would adapt to you or tables which would give you lectures in church history. The whole place was simple, unassuming and welcoming.

There were some books on the shelves, some familiar and many unfamiliar. They appeared to be mainly about church history. I picked out a small paperback and started reading about early church architecture. It was interesting, in a dry academic way. But I couldn't concentrate on it, so I slipped the book into my pocket to read later. I sat down to wait for Lydia and Petra to come back from wherever they had disappeared to.

When they came in, Petra clapped her hands together. 'Hi everyone,' she said. 'We've got some visitors, today. Lydia you know ...' There were murmurs of acknowledgement. 'And this is my grand ... er ... Nick.'

People smiled and said their 'hellos'. I think I waved my hand, but I was in a bit of a daze.

'Are you okay?' said Lydia.

'Not really,' I whispered. 'All the rest you showed me? That was okay. I could deal with that. That was technology and stories and theory. This ... Petra ... these people. My granddaughter. This is *real*.'

'Don't worry,' said Lydia. 'They don't know who you are. Only Petra and I know the truth. She's the only one I told.'

'Why did you bring me here?'

'Because every journey needs a destination,' she said. 'And every dark night needs the hope of dawn.'

After a few further minutes chatting, the young man who had been putting the cloth on the table disappeared into the kitchen, from where he immediately emerged carrying a tray of food which was shared around the group. There was bread and salads and fruit and we sat eating and talking. Or rather, the others did the talking. I was still too dazed to do anything other than listen to what people were saying.

Then – with no discernible break in the proceedings – this simple party, this ordinary shared meal, began to turn into a sort of church service.

It was very different to any service I'd ever been involved in. I suppose it was nearer to a house group than anything else – but a house group with a shared sense of sacred and a serious-ness of purpose. Most of the people contributed. An older woman gave a short talk about an answer to prayer that she'd received. Someone else read a passage from the Bible, and there was a short discussion. There was some singing – including some songs which were familiar to me and which were described by Petra as a few 'golden oldies'. A teenager opened a scruffy leather bag and pulled out a painting – at least I think it was a painting – it was an abstract mess of colours and textures, some of which seemed to shimmer and move like holograms. I couldn't really relate to it at all, but the others in the group asked questions, and the young girl explained why she'd painted it and what kinds of feelings she was trying to get across. Then there were prayers, both for the people in the group and for other groups that were mentioned. Someone opened an old book and read a few scraps of liturgy, familiar phrases, worn smooth by time, but still heavy with meaning.

Then a simple piece of bread was broken and shared, an old, chipped pottery mug of crimson wine was passed round the group, and the familiar, ancient words were spoken. However different the rest of the event had been, this at least I knew, and I felt the presence of God, as tangible as the bread, as warming as the wine.

Finally, Petra read a letter they'd been sent from a church near them, asking them for help. People discussed what they could do, and they agreed to send what money they could. Then Petra prayed for the group and the meeting ended.

In themselves, the elements were not so different to experiences from my time, but the combination of them all, the homeliness with which they were presented and the seriousness with which they were engaged in made them different and distinctive. I didn't understand all the words, and I didn't respond to every part of the service – but the sense of involvement and community was overwhelming. This small group were sharing; sharing food, sharing insight, sharing something sacred and holy. Whatever my thoughts about their 'service', this was something they had created and in which they were all intimately involved.

As the meeting closed some began to drift away, some helped to clear up. Gradually the room began to empty and I was left alone with my granddaughter.

There were so many questions I had for her; questions about her father – my son – and her aunts, my daughters. Questions about her own life. But somehow I sensed that she would not answer these enquiries. Those questions were not the point of my journey. So we talked about her church, the people and the service. She was joined by Jimmy – the lad who had been baking the bread earlier, who held her hand.

'Is it usually like this?' I asked.

'Sort of,' she replied. 'We're kind of a 24/7 church. Most nights people gather here. But we only do all this once a week.'

'I see. So who's the church leader?'

'Well, it's in my house,' she said, 'so I suppose I have responsibility for calling it together. But there isn't really a leader. Certainly no-one who's paid.'

'And does it always follow the same pattern?'

She laughed. 'Was there a pattern there? I didn't notice. No – things change. Some elements stay broadly the same, but mostly it's a question of what issues the followers need to discuss. We try to talk about what's bothering them, and share in what's exciting them. I guess we try to respond to what's actually happening in their lives at the moment. We try to balance the old elements of worship with something new. We might tell a story or listen to some poetry or . . . well, anything, really, that brings people closer to God.'

'It seemed very low-tech.'

'Low-tech?'

'You know. Nobody wore their Putershades, things were read out from letters, it was quite old-fashioned in its way. I felt almost at home.'

'Perhaps "timeless" would be a better word than "old-fashioned",' she giggled. 'I suppose we've just tried to make things accessible to people. You've seen the kind of people who live around here – I mean, they're not the kind of people who rate modern technology very highly. Some churches have really embraced the Virtuality thing and work in that mission field. We're kind of at the opposite end of the spectrum. Maybe that's just the style of this meeting. We're trying to get back towards something a little grittier; a little more . . .' she thought for a moment.

'Real,' suggested Jimmy.

'Yes,' agreed Petra. 'Or immediate. Or tactile. Yeah, maybe that's it. Isn't that all people want, really? Belief that's alive. A faith you can touch. Which is not to say we don't use the shades and all that. Just not in the context of the service itself.'

I looked around me at the room. Without the people in it, it looked quite shabby and rather bare.

'Where does the money come from to support the work?'

They both burst out laughing. 'What money?' giggled Jimmy. 'Is there some money that I haven't been told about?'

'Look, Granddad,' said Petra, suddenly serious. 'It's not like the old days here. We all work for a living. There are no buildings and no full-time staff – at least not in our group. Some groups have specialists who work among children or young people or different ethnic groups, but they are employed for their particular skills. There are no "general" leaders any more. There are people who teach and people who pastor and people who organise – but no-one who tries to do all those at once.' She laughed. 'What money we have, we give away.'

'And do you always have paintings?'

'No,' she said. 'But we always have art. People express themselves in different ways. Aruna loves art – it's the one thing that brings her alive. So we encourage that. Wherever people have a passion or a skill we try to help them use it in worship.'

'And who is in charge of the whole thing?'

'In charge?'

'Yes, you know,' I said. 'Who is the bishop or the general sec-retary or the director or something ...'

'Oh we gave up on all that,' she said. 'We don't have those kind of structures any more. There simply isn't the need for them or the people who want to be in them.'

'We're more like a network here,' said Jimmy. 'We have rela-tionships with the churches near us, and there is a big congrega-tion just across the river where we sometimes go to worship, but we're entirely self-governing.'

'But surely someone must guide you? Surely there are people who help with the strategic thinking, who organise the resources?'

'No, it's not that kind of thing any more,' insisted Petra. 'You keep thinking of the church like a warship, with a captain on the bridge and the crew obeying orders. But we're not an aircraft car-rier any more; we're a fleet. We're hundreds of little boats, going where they will, doing what they think is right.' She grinned. 'We're not the navy, you know. We're *pirates*!'

'Of course there are teachers we listen to,' said Jimmy. 'And each church is in a relationship with two of its neighbours to ensure accountability and support. But we don't have any cen-tralised leadership. We're a cloud of witnesses and you can't centralise a cloud.'

'So how many churches like this are there?' I asked.

'We're not exactly sure,' said Petra. 'They're a bit fluid; hard to keep track of. There's no bureaucracy, nobody administrating the whole thing. The churches keep moving to where the people are. One of the traps the church of your time fell into was always expecting the people to come to it; they had to come to your building. Well, we go to where the people are.' She gestured around her. 'We chose this house because it was near to Whitehall, so we could work among the homeless people there. Other groups have gone to different areas, and they do church in different ways. They do whatever they can to involve people.'

'I never realised. I got the impression from Lydia that the church was virtually dead now.'

'Oh, it is,' said Petra. 'In numbers anyway. We just woke up to the danger too late. But, you know, the one good thing about a near-death experience is that it makes you appreciate life so much more. So now we do things very differently. The church in the UK now is small in numbers but big in ideas. And God is doing amazing things through his church here. Then again, that's God for you. He loves bringing people back from the dead.'

'And are all churches like this?'

She looked shocked. 'Of course not. Bazzing heck, Granddad, haven't you learnt anything? They adapt themselves to the needs of the people in the group. Some still provide what you might call a "traditional" model. Some even meet in churches still. Some are much more music-based. Some are basically discussion groups with some prayer thrown in. Some offer a more social model, providing a range of services to people who need them. Like I said, some exist only in the Virtuality, building connections and relationships that way. Each one looks around for the right model. Every boat has a different design and a different way of sailing. So don't go back and tell people to do it our way. Tell them to go back and do what works.' She thought for a moment. 'And tell them to make sure that it's about real life. Our aim is to help people embody the values of Jesus. Real church begins when they walk out of the door.'

I looked at her. For the first time on my journey I felt a sense of optimism. If there were people like her, people committed to making Jesus real to those around them, then the church – however low the numbers – stood a chance. As she sat there next to Jimmy, I felt incredibly proud. She was a frail, fragile thing, this granddaughter I never knew I had, this girl wearing her too-big clothes and her naïve smile. But she had the strength of hope and the vigour of youth. She had what the church of my day needed so much: hope, faith, a determination to live out her faith, a deep-down, rooted conviction that what she believed *mattered*. As I stared at her, my eyes went misty. I could see a family likeness, she reminded me so much of her grandmother. I wiped my eyes. But strangely, they were still misty. My head suddenly started to spin.

'Granddad,' Petra said. 'What's wrong?'

I couldn't hold myself up and began to slump to the floor. Petra grabbed hold of me and stared down in alarm. 'Lydia!' she called. 'Something's happening!'

I was dimly aware of Lydia rushing into the room. She knelt over me and stared into my eyes.

'I think it's over,' she said to Petra. 'He's fading away.'

I struggled to speak.

'Must know ... one last thing ...' I stammered.

'What is it, Granddad?' asked Petra.

'How ... how did I die?'

Petra cradled me in her arms and looked down at me.

'You don't know?' she asked, quietly. 'Well, it was all to do with this water-buffalo and the firework display. What happened was ...'

But I could no longer hear her. Her features seemed to glow, they seemed to be diffused with light.

'You look ... ' I murmured, 'so like your grandmother ...'

Then there was a terrible rushing sound and a deep darkness and a thumping pain behind my eyes, and suddenly I found myself lying in bed, in my time, and looking up into the eyes of my wife.

'Hello,' she said, leaning over me. 'You're back.'

'You,' I said. 'You look just like your granddaughter.'

Dear Miles,

Thank you so much for your last letter. I am so relieved to know that our friendship is still intact. You have no idea how much your friendship means to me.

And your question is perfectly valid; if I didn't like the shape of the church I was in, what church would I have been happy in?

It's a good question – and I suppose it ties in with this section of the manuscript. The church described in Page's story hardly seems like anything particularly radical or special. I was struck with the everyday feel of it. (But then perhaps that attests to the truth of his tale? Maybe if he was making it all up he would have created something more exciting? Or maybe he would have visited a lot of different churches to get his point across?)

I suppose to be fair to him, the point is that there is no ideal model of church. There is only what works for different communities, people groups or environments.

However, I began this exercise by trying to identify some characteristics of the early church, so it makes for a pleasing symmetry that I should end it by trying to identify the defining elements of the future church.

Most of these ideas I have taken from looking at the society around me. It is a complex society, these days. We don't know whether to define people as Generation X, Generation Y, Postmodernists or Postmillennialists. But however you define them, they all think that the church belongs to the old way of doing things. So, what would a new church look like if we allowed these people to shape it?

I think the future church will be:

Small, but Powerful

Most Christian ministry throughout history has been a matter of small, potent, motivated groups. This will be the case in the future. Churches will be smaller, more energised, more intimate. There will be big churches, but they will resource small groups.

Passionately Committed

The church of the future will be passionately committed to the cause. It will have to be, otherwise it faces extinction. In the face of widespread apathy – and even opposition – it will be more costly to be a Christian, and it will demand more commitment.

Based around Relationships

Younger Christians place a higher value on relationships than they do on dogma or doctrine. Friendship is a sacred place. Doctrine and dogma has its place, but the church is a social reality as well as a theological one.

Explorative and Honest

People today distrust anyone who appears to have all the answers, be they politician, physician or priest.

Certainty is a dead end; but these people are on a journey. They prefer honest uncertainty to unquestioned faith. There will be mutual encouragement towards a real spirituality. People will explore, question, journey, share encounters.

Minimally Structured

Churches will have to have flat management structures, with a lot of consultation and interaction between the layers. People have no time for hierarchies or levels of authority. In politics, in business, even in criminal justice we are seeing authority and decision making devolved downwards. The same has to happen in churches.

Lightly Led

Unquestioned authority has had its day, and the more a church insists on it, the less response they will get. Respect has to be earned. And if it is true for people, it is also true for the 'authority of Scripture'. Scripture will be explored, listened to, engaged with, but perhaps not 'worshipped'. Its statements will be tested against reality.

Connected with Life

Churches will take their symbols, stories and language from real life. Christians want a '24/7 faith', not just one that is confined to Sundays. Similarly spirituality and teaching will honestly engage with real-life issues such as suffering and disability.

Holistic in Outlook

The church is part of the world. In the global village there must be a global parish church. Christianity has to be connected to world views and take in ecological dimensions. The church can no longer let its missionary organisations be its global arm. With the growth of the Internet and the ease of travel, churches will become their own mission agencies and will make connections to churches and organisations throughout the globe.

Missionary by Default

Mission will be part of the DNA of any future church. It will not be the optional extra that it is at the moment but would be a natural part of Christian life. But mission is more than traditional 'evangelism'; missionary lives will speak as well as missionary words.

Unafraid of Emotions

We are no longer the society of the stiff upper lip. Laughter and tears will be commonplace. The church will be a place of party as well as mourning; it will be a place of celebration and reflection. People want to feel something, not just think about things.

Full of Creativity

Spirituality will be expressed through a wide range of creative activities, not just through preaching, liturgy and music. Art, sculpture, photography, hobbies and interests will all be legitimate sources of spiritual enrichment.

Engaged with the Culture

The culture around the church will be allowed to inform and shape the expressions of worship and language. It will not be dismissed as shallow, evil or irrelevant.

Unburdened by Buildings

Buildings will be seen as relatively unimportant. Worship spaces will be flexible and intimate. A post-millennial sacred space might be a room or a warehouse or a forest glade.

A Place of Refuge

The church will be a place of refuge rather than a test of strength. It will reach out by grace to engage all layers of society. People will be able to belong, without having to believe all the right things.

———————

There. A fairly exhaustive, not to say exhausting, list, I am sure you'll agree! I could add a few more, but let's not be greedy. Anyway, few churches would be able to embody all of these facets, but most of them will simply have to embody most of the attributes if they are to exist at all.

In many ways we are back where we started. The early church must have been close to this. They might have had a different view of authority, and they may have had a greater emphasis on doctrine, but that comes of being a church that is in its infancy.

That, I think is as far as a man of my background and years can take it. Would I go to a church that embodied these principles? I think so. I might not find it the most comfortable place in the world, but then, who said church was supposed to be comfortable?

I'm nearly finished with the manuscript. It's fictional, of course. But then you knew that all along.

Ever yours,
Stephen

tHe eNd of tHe dReAm

12

'Where am I?'

'In hospital,' said my wife. 'We've not been here long. They've just brought you back. You were found in the square. The doctor is on his way ...'

'No,' I said. I looked around me wildly. A moment ago I had been in London, forty years into the future, finding out what was left of the church in the UK. Now I was lying in bed, staring at a ceiling that needed repainting and a bedside lamp that hadn't worked since about 1986.

'I've been away. I've been into the future. I spent days there. I met my granddaughter!' I stammered. 'The furniture talks to you and everyone goes to Bermuda via their sunglasses and snakes live in old Bible colleges and ... I've seen what's happened to the church.' I grabbed her arm suddenly, like a drowning man clutching onto a piece of driftwood. The purpose of my visit rose before me, as solid as a rock. 'Quick! We've got to do something. They're going to turn the church into sheltered housing!'

She smiled at me. 'Calm down,' she said. 'You haven't been anywhere. You were only found about an hour ago. You're confused.' She paused. 'That is, you're more confused than normal.'

'You don't realise. We are going to have a son . . .'

'Don't be ridiculous,' she said, simply. 'It's impossible, and I have the medical certificate to prove it.'

I tried to focus on her but found myself drifting off again into blackness.

→•←

Over the next few days I pieced together the story. I had got off the bus just as the storm broke. There had been a lightning strike in the square, and I'd been found lying on the ground by some friends who happened to be in the pub at the time. The ambulance – and my wife – had been called, and I was taken to the hospital in the next town. The lightning had struck me straight between the shoulders; Claire showed me the linen jacket I had been wearing, with a round, charred hole about the size of a cricket ball burned into the back.

'We'll take this home,' she said. 'We ought to frame it, to commemorate your adventure.'

When I 'woke' in hospital, it was only an hour after I'd been found – and yet in that time everything that had happened to me – the encounter with Lydia, the visit to London, the meeting with my granddaughter, all that I'd learnt of the future of the church – all those events had been compressed into one hour of blackness. It seemed that all I had experienced, all the sights, sounds, smells, all the vivid conversations and the painful encounters; all those had been nothing more than a dream; a lightning-charged hallucination. It wasn't long before I was passed fit to leave hospital – indeed, as far as the doctors could tell I had suffered no real ill-effects at all from the lightning strike. So I went home and tried to come to terms with what the dream meant.

Except that I couldn't come to terms with it; because I knew it wasn't a dream. I'm not sure why, or how, but I became convinced that, against all reasonable, rational, explanation, this was no dream. It had happened to me. I had been there. It wasn't a vision, it was a visit. In some way, in a way beyond my comprehension, I had been into the future. And now I had the task of telling others what I'd seen.

So, I began.

I explained to my friends, my family, to anyone who would listen, what had happened to me. I told them, as calmly as I could, that in forty years the church in the UK would effectively be invisible. I told them that I had travelled into the future, where I met a woman called Lydia who had originally been in my own church, in my own time. I explained that Lydia had taken me on a journey and that I had seen how close the church was to complete extinction. I told them that in some way, in defiance of medical opinion, my wife and I would have a son, whose daughter I would meet in the future.

The reaction was mixed, to say the least. Most people thought I was ill. Some thought that it was an elaborate practical joke or a desperate publicity stunt. People nodded politely, looked at their watches and realised that they'd forgotten a very important meeting and would I excuse them and they'd call back and see me when I was feeling up to it.

So I decided that if my friends wouldn't listen, I would make it 'public'. A few weeks after the incident, I was invited by a church in the nearby town to give a testimony entitled 'How I Was Hit by Lightning but Survived to Praise the Lord'. I prepared a measured, reasonable account, but, as I reached the stage and looked out at the sea of faces in front of me, something snapped.

'You're all doomed!' I shouted. 'You're all going towards oblivion! This place is a housing development waiting to happen!' Their faces fell. This was not the happy-clappy, warm and fluffy evangelistic moment they had been hoping for. In place of the safe Christian speaker they had booked, there was a wide-eyed lunatic on stage; a Jeremiah in jeans, wildly gesticulating and rambling on about interactive sunglasses. In the end I was 'helped' off stage by several stewards, the church caretaker and the vicar's dog, which assumed I was attacking him and bit me in the leg.

After this, I became a bit obsessed. I began to take every opportunity to talk about it. No, that's not quite right. I began to take every opportunity to rant about it. I didn't like what was happening to me. I could see my own family start to look at me with suspicion, their love and affection pushed to the very edge by my behaviour. You could tell that they were all given a fresh understanding of what Ezekiel's relatives had to go through. I was aware that, at times, I wasn't making sense, I was almost incoherent, and yet there was this feeling in me – so intense, so burning – that I couldn't keep bottled up. It couldn't go on, of course. The last straw came when I sent a detailed account of my journey to the future to *Christianity & Renewal* magazine, only to have the editor print it as fiction.

In the end, an old friend was delegated to meet with me and 'talk it through'. I loved Miles. He was the vicar of a church near my old hometown. I had known him for twenty years. I trusted him, looked up to him. Tall, scruffy, with sandy hair that never did what his wife wanted it to, full of love, gentle, always with time for anyone, always thinking of new ways to care for people; in a way he *was* the church for me.

'Hasn't this gone far enough, Nick?' he asked. 'People are laughing at you.' He was sitting by my bed. I was lying there, listless, apathetic, worn-out by the fever of all I had seen.

'Shame. And they always took me so seriously before. Anyway, they always mock the prophets of the Lord.'

'You're not a prophet of the Lord. You're a balding middle-aged hack with a bee in his bonnet. Don't get ideas above your station.'

I smiled. 'Okay. Maybe I'm not a prophet of the Lord. But I've *seen* things, Miles.' I sat up and gripped his arm. 'I've been to the future, and I've seen what was left of the church. It's all going, Miles. We're going to lose it all.'

'I've read the stories, Nick,' he said quietly. 'There's no need to start shouting.'

I lay back on the bed. 'Well, then. You get the point.'

'No,' he said. 'All I "get" is mindless panic. All I can see is a man I love burning himself out in alarm. Do you want us to panic?'

There was a silence. 'Panic is better than apathy,' I said. 'At least in a panic some people might escape. The church is doomed, Miles.'

Miles just waved his hand.

'I can see what you're saying, Nick,' he replied. 'But let's be honest, you've always been this way. You're always moaning about the church, being negative, knocking things. You enjoy it. You'd be lost without the church to kick about.'

'Is that how it's come across?'

'Yes,' he said. 'That's how it came across. Oh, you were funny, of course. But you've always been antichurch.'

I sighed. 'I don't mean to. I'm not antichurch. And I know that there are lots of good things happening all around. I have friends, people like you, Miles, who are doing church in radical ways, who are building great communities. There are loads of good things happening in the church, of course there are. There are lots of churches who are trying new ways of communicating.

Loads of Christians who are working hard to make their faith real.'

'So why don't you talk about them? Why didn't you write about them if you wanted to get your point across?'

'Because that's not what I saw. Because they've already got the message. Because there are thousands of churches who aren't listening.'

'You don't know that. You can't be sure.' He took off his glasses, rubbed them on his jumper and put them back on. They looked dustier than ever. 'Well, I'm not going to sit here and argue about statistics. Of course we're going through difficult times. But that's all the more reason to keep optimistic and keep the faith.'

'How are we going to keep the faith if there is no-one left to keep it?'

'Oh don't be ridiculous!' he exploded, and for the first time he looked angry. 'It's nonsense to talk of the church disappearing. It's part of the fabric of our society.'

'Society is changing, Miles,' I said. 'In fact, society has changed. Or haven't you noticed? You only think that it will survive because, so far, it has survived. You think that, because it's the "established" church that its future is guaranteed. But there are no guarantees any more. Who is to say that the monarchy will survive the next twenty-five years? And if there are questions about them, then how much more are there questions about the church?'

He looked at me and smiled. Unconvinced. 'What do you want?'

'I want the church to act. I want it to change, to adapt, to shake the future, before the future breaks it. I want the church to be a lion. Not an ostrich. I want it to get angry about things, to get passionate. I want it to feel things instead of just think about them. I want it ... oh, I don't know. I just want it to stop dying, to start living again.' My shoulders sagged with the weight of emotion. 'I've been to the future, Miles.'

'So you say.' He looked at me sadly.

'You don't believe my story ...'

'I believe that you believe it.'

I looked down and noticed my hands were trembling. 'Look, Miles,' I said. 'Whatever you think of me, of my story, whether you think it was dream or reality, I think it happened for a purpose. I think we still have a chance. The future is not fixed. We can change things.'

'You have the solution, then?'

'No. Of course not. But I know one thing. We have to start with the children. If you want to change the future you have to start with those who are going to build that future. If I had one message to the church today, I'd say, "start young". Turn all your resources, all your efforts on engaging and discipling young people. They are the ones who can change the future. And they're the ones who are leaving the church in the biggest numbers.' I smiled. 'That's how all this started, you see ... I was thinking about my daughters. I don't want them left without anyone to introduce them to Jesus ...'

'They've always got you.'

'Oh yeah,' I shrugged. 'They've got me.' I looked up at him. 'But I'm burnt out, Miles, haven't you noticed. I went too high and burnt up on re-entry. I'm just so tired ...'

Suddenly I found myself crying, weeping for the future, weeping for the disintegration of the past. The tension, the fear, the bewildering uncertainty were weighing so heavily on me. I just couldn't take it anymore.

Then I felt Miles's arms around me, steadying me, holding me like an anchor. I felt him reach out and pull me back from the abyss. And in that moment he was the rock, he was the church, he was the haven in all the storms. I clung to him and cried.

'You know what I think?' he said, at last. 'I think people are not meant to time-travel.' He looked into my red-rimmed eyes. 'It's messed you up, Nick. It's time to come home.'

After that, things were calmer. I still had flashbacks. I still had vivid visions, of a woman in silver, of a church that was a museum, of all the things I had seen. There were times when I could see doors in churches; when the traffic faded away to be replaced by ghostly, floating eggs. But I began to step back from it all. I even began to think that maybe these people were right. Maybe I dreamt it all. Maybe it was just the lightning flash and the impact of my all-too-soft head on the all-too-hard flagstones of the village square. It was a dream. It *had* to have been a dream.

Then two things happened. Six months later I was back preaching in my church again. The PCC had voted to allow me to preach, on the strict provision that I didn't mention the words 'church' or 'extinct' or 'we're all doomed, I tell you, doomed'. After the sermon, I met a new family who had crept in at the back, a mother who had moved out of London with her daughter. She was a teacher. She liked the community, liked the people. Something about her looked familiar. Those blue eyes, that determined stare. It couldn't be, could it?

'My name's Sharon,' she said.

I breathed a sigh of relief.

'What's the matter?' she asked. 'You look like you've seen a ghost.'

'No, it's just . . . it's just you remind me of someone I once knew. Or will know. But it's not you.'

She looked confused. Then she decided to ignore it.

'Anyway,' she said. 'I must be going.' And suddenly emerging from behind her was a smaller, younger copy; her daughter. The same blue eyes, the same stare, the same expression. 'This is my daughter,' said Sharon.

'Hi,' said the girl. 'My name's Lydia.'

With those few words, the wall I had carefully built up crumbled. It was her. It was Lydia. I knew then that everything I'd experienced was real. In forty years time I would be sitting in the same place talking to her and drinking tea. But we would be in a house, not a church.

And suddenly, as the wall crumbled, another memory was revealed. I remembered something. Muttering my apologies to the girl and her mother, I rushed home, raced upstairs and threw open the wardrobe doors. There, hanging forlornly at the back, was the jacket, still hanging there, its fabric scorched with the fury of the lightning strike. Surely there would be some proof in here; something I'd forgotten. I pulled it off the hanger and, as I did so, something fell out with a dull thud. It was a small green book; the book I had started to read in Petra's lounge just before the service. I picked it up and looked at the title: *Churches and Homes: The Effect of the Domestic Setting on the Worship of the Early Church.* By S. Thornton. I looked inside. 'First published 2010.'

I can't remember much more of that day. I know that I spent it walking up and down the streets of the village, crossing the fields, wandering, lost in a daze. I know that I felt lost, abandoned, alone. There was no-one who could understand me, no-one who could reach into my loneliness and pull me out.

Make that *almost* no-one. It was my wife who found me. I was sitting on a bench in the village square. It was raining and my clothes were soaked. Everything was grey. I was still clutching the book, which had turned into a soggy mass of pulp in my hands.

'Hello,' she said. She sat down beside me and took my hand. 'I've been worried about you.'

'It's all true,' I whispered. 'I've seen her.'

'Who?'

'Lydia.' I held up the soaking wad of paper. 'And this – I brought this back.'

She just shrugged.

'You know your problem?' she said. 'You talk too much.' She smiled. 'You talk too much and write too much and you don't do enough. Oh, it's easy enough to blame the church for the mess, but let's face it, the church is only a group of people. It's individuals who make the difference.'

'What are you saying?'

'I'm saying that instead of moaning about church, maybe you should start fixing it.'

'But what can I do?'

'I don't know. You'll think of something. I just think the time for talking is at an end.'

I nodded. Drops of rain fell off my nose and splashed onto my hands.

'Okay,' I said. 'Point made.'

She held my hand. 'Sooner or later you, me, everyone, we have to start taking action,' she said. She sounded urgent.

'What's brought this on?' I said. 'I thought you didn't believe me ...'

'Well,' she said. 'We've got to think of the children. I don't want my granddaughter to be running the only church in London.'

'You mean . . .'

She nodded.

'I'm pregnant,' she said.

Dear Miles,

I asked for a shock from God. Maybe I should have kept my mouth shut.

When Caroline died I was working on a book. I had the title sorted and the main argument. I had got about halfway through the writing, but after C's death I stopped writing and put it in the bottom drawer of my desk.

And there it remains. No-one knows about it. Even Caroline only knew that I was working on something.

I have the title page in front of me: it's called *Churches and Homes: The Effect of the Domestic Setting on the Worship of the Early Church*.

I don't understand it. No-one knows about this. So how come Page refers to it? How come he knows the title and the subject?

I thought the story was a fake. I was *sure* it was a fake. It was. Wasn't it?

Yours,
Stephen Thornton

QuestioNs

The following questions were found in a notebook in Nick Page's possession after he returned from his journey. He appears to have been listing questions to help churches think through some of the issues his journey raises, and some of the things they have to think about in the future.

They have been reordered to tie in with the chapters of his manuscript.

1. A Nasty Shock

1. Do I know what is happening in my church? Is it growing or declining?
2. Do I know what the picture is in my denomination? What steps are the leadership taking?
3. If there were no church in my town, village or community, what would that mean? What difference would it make?

2. Dead Again

1. Lydia said 'that was one of the main things the church had to teach people: what it meant to keep promises.' What does this mean for us?

2. How are we supposed to be different? And how are we supposed to be walking images of God?

3. Are there times when instead of making people feel welcome we make them feel guilty? How do we make sure we are giving bread and not stones?

3. The Living Museum

1. Does my church have traditions? If so, are they helpful?

2. Do our services give people a pattern or rhythm to their lives. Does this matter any more?

3. 'Art is important. Beauty is important.' Is this true? If so, what is my church doing in these areas?

4. Do people understand our services? Do we explain the language we are using?

4. The Archbishop

1. Does my church have structures which help or hinder its mission? Do our church structures empower people?

2. Are we building teams or just making committees?

3. Do we appoint 'safe' people to posts? Does our appointment system reward good behaviour or give people the chance to shine?

4. How are decisions taken in the church? Are they fast and efficient, or does everything take ages?

5. What do we want out of our denomination now? What resources could it be providing?

5. The Boiled Lobster

1. What skills do you need to run a church? How many of these are 'management' skills?

2. Has the church got a clear vision of where it is going?
3. Is there a good balance between 'theology' and practice in our church? Or are we just learning things we don't need to know?
4. Do we scan the environment? What great ideas from outside the church have we taken and adapted for our use?
5. Are there people in the church who should be given the chance to gain hands on experience now?

6. Physician, Heal Yourself

1. How many of my church are engaged in public service? How can I support them better?
2. How can my church practically care for our community?
3. How can we ensure that people feel cared for and loved?
4. Do I actually listen to people who talk to me? Or am I merely waiting for the opportunity to speak?

7. The Set Menu

1. Does my church do the same thing each week?
2. How many people attend? Are we a cell church without realising it?
3. How can we offer more variety in our services?
4. Have we actually asked what people want from our church? How do we consult them?
5. What small groups could serve our community? What kinds of things could they offer?
6. Are there other forms of church from which we could learn, or other networks that we ought to be serving?

8. Life's a Beach

1. In what ways does my church reach out to the community?
2. How could we make better contact with those who are locked into their own worlds?
3. Does my church embody the teachings of Jesus? Or do we just talk about them a lot?
4. What does it mean to love our neighbour in today's society? Who is our neighbour anyway?

9. A Visit to the Circus

1. What language do we use when talking about Christianity? Is it accessible?
2. Are there images or symbols which would get the point across better?
3. What would best communicate to the people around us? Should we be using entirely different methods and words?
4. Are there words or phrases – or even actions – in our church that are completely incomprehensible to the outsider?
5. Are we sure that the congregation actually understand the words?

10. Real Life

1. How is teaching done in my church?
2. Are there ways to make the teaching more relevant?
3. What subjects do people need to know about that we aren't covering?

4. Are there people with special needs or requirements in the church? What kind of teaching or resources might help them?
5. Do our church services help people with their real life? Are we helping them to be Christians 24/7?

11. A Visit to Church

1. What kind of church would I like to see in my community?
2. Are we a welcoming church? Or are people put off by us?
3. What is the atmosphere like in church?
4. What can be done to ensure that visiting the church is a positive, warm experience?
5. Is everyone involved in our services? If not, how could we involve more people?

12. The End of the Dream

1. What can I do to help the church at the moment?
2. Do I just complain about things? Or am I ready to get my hands dirty?
3. How can we make changes in a positive way in the church today?

biBliogRaphy aNd fuRtheR resouRces

Print

Brierley, P. (2000). *Steps to the future: what we need to know before we can think strategically about the church's future in Britain.* London, Christian Research and Scripture Union.

Brierley, P. W. and Christian Research. (2000). *The tide is running out : what the English Church Attendance Survey reveals.* London, Christian Research.

Brierley, P. W. (2003). *UKCH religious trends.* London, Christian Research.

Brown, C. G. (2001). *The death of Christian Britain : understanding secularisation 1800–2000.* London, Routledge.

Church of England. (2000). *Common worship : services and prayers for the Church of England.* London, Church House Publishing.

Church of England. (2002). *Common worship : daily prayer.* London, Church House Publishing.

Croft, S. J. L. (2002). *Transforming communities : re-imagining the church for the 21st century.* London, Darton Longman & Todd.

Cross, F. L. and E. A. Livingstone (1974). *The Oxford Dictionary of the Christian Church.* London, Oxford University Press.

Drane, J. W. (1997). *Faith in a changing culture : creating churches for the next century.* London, Marshall Pickering.

Drane, J. W. (2000). *The McDonaldization of the church : spirituality, creativity, and the future of the church.* London, Darton Longman & Todd.

Ellul, J. and O. Wyon (1951). *The presence of the Kingdom*. London, SCM Press.

Ellul, J. and J. Wilkinson (1964). *The technological society*. New York, Vintage Books.

Ellul, J. (1991). *Anarchy and Christianity*. Grand Rapids, Mich, William B. Eerdmans.

Ferguson, E., M. P. McHugh, et al. (1997). *Encyclopedia of early Christianity*. New York; London, Garland.

Gibbs, E. and I. Coffey (2001). *Church next : quantum changes in Christian ministry*. Leicester, Inter-Varsity.

Gill, R. (1988). *Beyond decline : a challenge to the churches*. London, SCM.

Gill, R. (2002). *Changing worlds*. Edinburgh, T & T Clark.

Green, M. (2002). *Church without walls : a global examination of cell church*. Carlisle, Paternoster.

Hopkins, K. (1999). *A world full of gods : pagans, Jews and Christians in the Roman Empire*. London, Weidenfield and Nicholson.

Hurtado, L. (2000). *At the origins of Christian worship: the context and character of earliest Christian devotion*. Carlisle, Paternoster Press.

Jackson, B. (2002). *Hope for the church : contemporary strategies for growth*. London, Church House.

Lings, G. & Murray, S. (2002). *Church planting – past, present and future*. Cambridge, Grove Books.

Marshall, I. H. (1980). *Last Supper and Lord's Supper*. Exeter, Paternoster Press.

McKechnie, P. (2001). *The first Christian centuries : perspectives on the early Church*. Leicester, Apollos.

Meeks, W. A. (1983). *The first urban Christians : the social world of the Apostle Paul*. New Haven; London, Yale University Press.

Moynagh, M. and Administry. (2001). *Changing world, changing Church : new forms of church, out-of-the-pew thinking, initiatives that work*. London, Monarch Books.

Murray, S. & Wilkinson-Hayes, A. (2000). *Hope from the margins – new ways of being church*. Cambridge, Grove Books.

Potter, P. (2001). *The challenge of cell church : getting to grips with cell church values*. Oxford, Bible Reading Fellowship.

Rhodes, D. (1996). *Cell church or traditional? : reflections on church growth in Mongolia.* Cambridge, Grove Books.

Thornton, S. (2010). *Churches and homes: the effect of the domestic setting on the worship of the early church.* Oxford, Subditivus Press.

Thorpe, K. (1997). *Doing things differently – Changing the heart of the church.* Cambridge, Grove Books.

Tidball, D. (1997). *The social context of the New Testament.* Carlisle, Paternoster.

Tomlin, G. and Society for Promoting Christian Knowledge (Great Britain) (2002). *The provocative church.* London, SPCK.

Warner, R. (1994). *21st century church.* London, Hodder & Stoughton.

Warren, R. and Church of England Board of Mission. (1995). *Building missionary congregations.* London, Church House.

Warren, Y. (2002). *The cracked pot : the state of today's Anglican parish clergy.* Stowmarket, Kevin Mayhew.

White, L. M. (1990). *Building God's house in the Roman world : architectural adaptation among pagans, Jews, and Christians.* Baltimore; London, Johns Hopkins University Press.

Websites

The following websites have some excellent resources:

Encounters on the Edge
A wide range of articles and resources covering emerging forms of churches
www.encountersontheedge.org.uk

Alternative Worship
Ideas and resources for alternative worship services
www.alternativeworship.org

Christian Research UK
All the statistics you could ever need . . .
www.christian-research.org.uk

CellUK Online

An organisation which encourages the promotion and development
of cell churches throughout the UK
www.cellchurch.co.uk

Springboard

The Archbishop's Initiative for Evangelism
www.springboard.uk.net

The Net

Network church in Huddersfield
www.netchurch.org.uk

Anglican Church Planting Initiatives

Providing advice, coaching and consultancy to Anglicans and other
denominations on Planting Churches, mission projects, church
growth and leadership
www.acpi.org.uk

Grove Books Online

A massive collection of useful books – the Evangelism section has lots
of relevant material
www.grovebooks.co.uk

Denominational Websites

Church of England

www.cofe.anglican.org

Church of Wales

www.churchinwales.org.uk

Scottish Episcopal Church

www.scotland.anglican.org

Catholic Church in England and Wales

www.catholic-ew.org.uk

Catholic Church in Scotland
www.catholic-scotland.org.uk/index.html

Church of Scotland
www.churchofscotland.org.uk

Methodist Church
www.methodist.org.uk

Baptist Union
www.baptist.org.uk

United Reformed Church
www.urc.org.uk

Salvation Army
www.salvationarmy.org.uk

Greek Orthodox
www.nostos.com/church/

Russian Orthodox
www.russian-orthodox-church.org.ru/en.htm

Religious Society of Friends
www.quaker.org

Author Biographies

Nick Page is a writer, information designer and creative consultant. He is the author of over twenty books including *The Tabloid Bible, The Bible Book, Lord Minimus* and *Blue*. He writes regularly for magazines such as *Youthwork* and *Christianity* and works for a number of charities and NGOs. He lives in Oxfordshire with his wife and three children. He supports Watford Football Club, but someone has to.

Stephen Thornton was Professor of Early Church History at Zion College Oxford. He is the author of many academic works including *A Dictionary of Early Church Legends*, *'A People of Flame': The First Christians in Ancient Hyperborea* and *Faith or Fake: Forged Documents in the Early Church*. He retired in 2001 and lives near Oxford. He never gives interviews.

Blue

Nick Page

Responding to the rapid growth of all things spiritual, Nick Page explores why the green issues of the 1990s are giving way to the blue issues of the New Millennium. According to market research experts Young and Rubicam, the colour of the next decade is blue. This is because more and more people are concerned with questions that are not material: better relationships, quality of life, rest and relaxation, life beyond ourselves. *Blue* explores why this new quest for a fuller life has come about, and what everyone can do to find greater personal fulfilment. In a popular and entertaining way, this unique book touches the deeper spiritual needs in everyone. The colour blue has come of age.

Softcover: 0-551-03265-0

Pick up a copy today at your favorite bookstore!

GRAND RAPIDS, MICHIGAN 49530 USA

WWW.ZONDERVAN.COM

We want to hear from you. Please send your comments about this book to us in care of zreview@zondervan.com. Thank you.

GRAND RAPIDS, MICHIGAN 49530 USA

WWW.ZONDERVAN.COM